Granny Hooks a Crook

A Fuschia Minnesota Mystery

by

Julie Seedorf

This book is fiction. All characters, events, and organizations portrayed in this novel are the product of the author's imagination or are used fictitiously. Any resemblance to actual persons—living or dead—is entirely coincidental.

Copyright © 2013 by Julie Seedorf

All rights reserved. No parts of this book may be reproduced or transmitted in any form or by any means, electronic or mechanical, including photocopying, recording or by any information storage and retrieval system, without written permission from the author, except for the inclusion of brief quotations in a review.

For information, email **Cozy Cat Press**, cozycatpress@aol.com or visit our website at: www.cozycatpress.com

COZY CAT PRESS

ISBN: 978-1-939816-12-2
Printed in the United States of America

Cover design by Laura Redmond
http:/www.lauradawnsky.info

1 2 3 4 5 6 7 8 9 10

I dedicate this book to my grandchildren, Abby, Brady, Maggie and Jake, who helped me find the forgotten child hidden inside of me and taught me how to play and dream again. Seeing the world anew through a child's eyes is the best inspiration of all.

Chapter One

Granny didn't always like to get up in the morning. It seemed a waste of a good bed to get out of it so early in the morning. First, Granny would wallow in the warmth. She would squirm a little and enjoy the softness of the mattress. Granny would then open one eye to see if it was light yet. If it appeared that the sun was up, she would open the other eye very slowly, not wanting to get too excited. Getting up too fast always made her head spin.

Granny would then stick her big toe out of the blanket, trying to determine the weather. Her big toe was a good barometer. If it started turning blue, she knew it was cold and her toe was going to throb on and off for the day. If it stayed red, Granny knew that it would be a good day for her flip flops, even though she wasn't supposed to be wearing them. Her kids harassed her about wearing her flip flops, something about not walking properly and being at risk of falling. She couldn't make them understand that at her age she was always at risk for falling, so why not live dangerously in her flip flops.

Granny always looked around first before attempting the final lift out of her bed. She had to make sure there weren't any kids or grandkids visiting before she threw off the covers. At her age it was easy to forget if her kids and grandkids had stayed over. Occasionally, she forgot they were there even before she climbed into bed. It didn't bother her that her memory was a little foggy. It was a good excuse to use when she needed to get out of something she didn't want to do, or if she got caught somewhere she wasn't supposed to be.

Usually, if Granny remembered before she went to bed that her kids and grandkids stayed over, she would dress in her granny gown pajamas. It was what they expected of someone her age and she didn't want to ruin their expectations. But when Granny was by herself, she occasionally slept in the nude and occasionally she wore her hot pink, silk shortie nightgown with red hearts on it. Or she might wear her purple leather PJ's that stated *Sexy Granny and I Know It*.

Granny's secret PJ's always made her smile before she went to bed. It made the creaky body and the saggy skin feel better. She still felt like that sexy granny inside. Her mind never did keep up with her body.

There were times her kids would visit unexpectedly in the morning and have breakfast waiting for Granny when she stumbled into the kitchen from her warm bed. She could see the horror on their faces if they caught her in anything other than her granny pajamas. She would be sent to the wrinkle farm faster than she could lose her flip flops.

Granny peered down the hall and listened carefully to see if there were live people in her house. She took the time to wonder what would happen if her kids and grandkids knew about her secret life. What would they do if they knew about her undercover work? Granny shuddered at the thought, decided she had the house to herself so she was safe in her purple leather and flip-flops and shuffled down the hallway to the kitchen.

Granny loved her cheery kitchen. She had painted it bright yellow when she had moved in all those years ago after her husband had died. With three children to raise, Granny felt yellow was the only color that could lift her spirits and remind her that in spite of the responsibility that was now hers, the sun would shine again in their lives.

The kitchen, located at the front of the house, had large windows that looked out onto the neighborhood. It was an old house located on the side of the block that was original to Fuchsia. When Granny first saw the house, she knew it had to be hers, with its large lawn and not too many neighbors close by. When the new housing started to go up across the street a few years later, she was worried that her privacy was going to be corrupted. What she found out was that having neighbors close by added some spice to her life because of their quirkiness.

Granny would have liked to change the outside of the house a little more. It was very respectfully painted a light gray with white trim. The ginger board at its peaks was a darker shade of gray outlined in white. The white porch on the front of the house was adorned with white wicker furniture along with a comfy white wooden swing hanging from its ceiling.

Granny had thought about painting the outside of the house when she first moved in to town in Fuchsia. Granny had toyed with the idea of painting it the color fuchsia to honor the town and topping the house off with purple trim. Older Victorian homes used to be more dramatic in color than boring gray, but Granny decided to leave it alone as her kids still needed to be raised and she had promised her dear, departed, dead husband to raise them up in the way they should go and so she did. Her only concession was to make sure that the porch was lined with potted Fuchsias in the summertime and colored lights in the wintertime. She also, on a whim, put a life-sized statue of the cartoon character Maxine outside her door. Maxine was her idol and she hoped to live up to Maxine's wit and uniqueness.

The first thing Granny did when she reached the kitchen was to pull out her binoculars and head to the window. Her neighbor Mavis was old and someone needed to check to see if she had kicked the bucket during the night. Mavis had a thing about shades on her windows. She didn't like them. Mavis claimed she didn't have anything to hide but Granny wondered if she just liked people watching her. Granny asked Mavis about that once and Mavis told her she had always wanted to be in a reality show on TV and this was the closest she was ever going to get to it.

The problem with Mavis not having shades on her window was that it was not easy to check on her. Sally, down the street, would pull her shade up in the morning so Granny knew she was ok. George, on the other end of the street, hung a pair of boxer shorts on the pole outside his door so Granny knew he was still alive and kicking. But Mavis, living straight across the street from Granny refused to do that, so Granny had to get out her binoculars and peer into Mavis's window to see if she could see Mavis moving around.

Granny secretly thought Mavis enjoyed this and it was a pretend part of Mavis's reality fantasy, because every time Granny would find

Mavis, it would seem Mavis was posing or acting out for the binoculars.

Yep, there she was. It was Mavis all right, all in her glory, in her mind-induced reality show. Mavis was hanging from the chandelier with one hand and waving to Granny with the other. If Mavis's children could see her now they would certainly think Mavis was losing her marbles. What they didn't know was that Mavis was always a little daring, a quirk she had kept hidden from her family. George's boxer shorts were hung on the pole. Today's shorts were covered with hearts. Granny decided she didn't want to know what that might mean. Sally had her shade pulled up. All was fine with her neighbors.

Granny proceeded on to her next task.

Chapter Two

Fish needed to be fed. Fish was the cat Granny rescued from a fish tank at the pet store. She happened to be walking by the fish tank at the pet store when she felt water hit her face. Looking closer at the tank, she found a huge alley cat floundering in the fish tank. When Granny reached in to save him, he thanked her by tattooing her arm red with his claws. Granny then and there knew that this cat was the cat for her.

Granny took the cat to the employees to purchase him and the employees informed her that this cat was free. He didn't belong to the pet store. He snuck in every day and tried to fish out the fish from the fish tank. Occasionally, he would crawl in and have to be rescued. They would be glad to be rid of him. Granny promptly named him Fish and took him home.

Fish had a personality of his own. He was feisty, lovable and was always bringing a new and unique present home for Granny to see. One night he thought Granny needed a new bra. Fish was aware of her nighttime attire. Who would have thought a cat could notice what someone wore. Fish, in his wandering, brought Granny home a hot pink, polka dot, padded bra. The only problem was that it was a 40DD. Granny could have only wished for those kinds of assets.

Fish was not your average looking hulk of an alley cat. Somewhere along the way, Fish had lost part of his tail, part of one of his ears and part of a paw. He was an unusual looking guy and when he pose, he looked as if he'd been out on an all night alley catter binge. He always looked a little tipsy.

Fish used the cat door most nights to wander around the town. Granny didn't worry about him. Before she left for her day, she would leave his food in his bowl and when she got home Fish would be waiting for her along with the latest present he had acquired for Granny.

As Granny put the food in the dish, she spied some leftover chocolate truffles that she had quickly hid underneath Fish's water bowl one evening when her eldest daughter had dropped in unexpectedly just as Granny was going to savor a delicious bite of the truffles for her dinner.

Granny lifted the bowl sneakily so Fish wouldn't see that there were chocolates within his reach. For some reason, Fish could sniff out anything but chocolate so Granny's hiding place was safe, not only from Fish, but from anyone else who might be snooping around. She grabbed the chocolate, warmed her coffee from the day before, dropped two sugar cubes in the coffee for energy and plopped into a chair by the window so she could run surveillance of the neighborhood before she left for her other creative endeavors.

Yes, life was good. Who would have thought that she, Hermiony Vidalia Criony Fiddlestadt, would finally have her life to herself. Granny looked down at her flip flops and fingered the words *Sexy Granny and I Know It* on the front of her PJ's as she became lost in thought.

"Hermiony, Hermiony" her mother used to call. Just when Hermiony was making progress in her quest to hunt down the thief who kept stealing her apples out of the hiding place in her tree in her parent's orchard. Her mother would call and Hermiony would have to go back to her boring homework and her boring chores around the house. "Hermiony," her mother would chastise her, "look at how you are dressed. A proper lady doesn't dress like a hooligan and run around out in the woods making up stories about someone stealing the apples out of our orchard." Hermiony didn't think her patched jeans and old t-shirt that she borrowed from her brothers would qualify as church dress but how could she climb trees and wade in the crick if she wore shoes and girl clothes all the time.

Hermiony would always answer, "Yes, mother." Then Hermiony would proceed to do as her mother said. As she got older, Hermiony would forget about her orchard adventures and settle into doing what her parents expected her to do. But before she became the good daughter Hermiony, she fixed the apple orchard thief. She didn't say, "I told you so" to her parents when they found Herman Picnic at the bottom of an apple tree one morning, right next to the wagon filled with the apples he had stolen the night before. Her mother and father couldn't figure out how the ground underneath one of the wagon wheels had sunk so fast that it threw Herman onto the ground beneath the tree with a broken leg so he couldn't get away when he was trying to abscond with the apples.

Granny smiled now as she was remembering the confusion on all the faces of the adults. They never did find the shovels she and her brothers had used to make the trap. She had had to blackmail her brothers into helping her but it was a small price for her brothers to pay so their parents wouldn't find out that they had been the ones who had rigged the water bucket to fall on Johnny Hedges' head at the Halloween dance that year.

No one had called Granny, Hermiony, in a long time. Her real name was another one of Granny's secrets. She could still hear the kids teasing her with the name "Hermiony Crybaby" over and over again. Those same teasers found snakes living in their lockers at school. No one would suspect Hermiony, since she had to act like the perfect lady that her parents wanted her to be and she pulled off the charade well. In fact, far from hooligan clothes, Hermiony was always the most put together dresser in the class. Why she was even voted best dressed girl her senior year in high school. Hermiony was also voted most likely to succeed as a designer in the fashion world, when she told everyone that being a fashion designer was a lifelong dream. Secretly, she thought she should design for Risque Secrets of the Bedroom fashion magazine but that wouldn't have been "proper."

Hermiony remembered asking her mother, "Why did you name me Hermiony, especially with a last name like Criony?" Her mother always replied, "I was in a rhyming phrase. I love to make up rhymes." Granny knew her mother stayed in that stage for a while because her brother was named Briony Criony. Then along came her younger brother Abraham. Neither she nor Briany could figure that one out so they had to ask their mom. "What happened to the rhymes?

"I fell in love with history. All of a sudden I loved Abraham Lincoln. I went from rhyme to time, history time and I didn't care if it was a rhyme." Her mother answered them with a far off look in her eyes. All Hermiony and Briany could do was roll their eyes and hope adulthood came soon so they could change their names.

Granny savored the last bit of chocolate as she came out of her reverie. She slurped down the left over coffee and went back to her bedroom to throw on some clothes for the day. She grabbed her Granny sweater, made a quick jump into her double knit polyester skirt, put on her hose stockings, tossed off her flip flops and put on her shoes and sprinted to the living room as exercise to loosen up before she became her undercover persona.

Granny glanced around her home to make sure she hadn't left any of her night clothes out in case her kids stopped by and let themselves in with their keys. Maybe it was time to take their keys away.

Granny grabbed her umbrella, put on her hat, pulled down the hose on her legs so she looked the way old ladies were expected to look, pulled out strands on her hair under her hat and locked the door on her way out.

Granny walked across the lawn and opened her garage door. She paused as she opened the door to let her eyes roam around the neighborhood, making sure no one was tinkering with any of the garbage that was sitting on the street waiting to be collected by Gorgonzo Garbage. She put one foot into her garage and stopped. Her garage was empty. There was no red 1957 Chevy Corvette convertible standing in front of her. Where had she left her car this time? It wasn't unusual for Granny to misplace her convertible. Downtown Fuschia wasn't too far away, just a mile or two as the crows flies, and if she was deep in thought she would forget that she drove to town. There were times she would forget that she owned a red 1957 Chevy Corvette. It was part of Granny's foggy memory. She didn't worry about it. If she did start to worry she would forget what she was worrying about.

Granny hurried out of the garage. She would be late for work if she didn't step it up. It was lucky Granny wore her red, sparkly, high top tennis shoes. They seemed to help her walk faster and if she got tired, she would use her umbrella as a cane to lean on.

Granny always enjoyed a good walk into town. Usually she would take the time to sing a song to Mrs. Shrill's hound, Baskerville, down the way, along Granny's trek into town. Baskerville always joined in on the chorus.

Mrs. Shrill would come out of her house and give Granny one of those "tut, tut, tuts" and wag her finger at Granny before she dragged Baskerville into the house. Granny would skip on down the street laughing.

Baskerville was one big dog. He was a mix between a bloodhound and a mastiff. He had the most soulful, bloodshot eyes that could melt anyone's heart with one look, except Mrs.

Shrills. His large Mastiff nose and head seemed a little off with his long dangly ears. His howls could be heard all across town when he was unhappy. Granny had often thought of sneaking him away one night and having him howl in the cemetery behind her house as she was telling ghost stories to the kids that came to her house on Halloween. She would really hear the "tut, tut, tuts" from Mrs. Shrill then. Granny smiled her mischievous grin as she thought of all the ruckus that would cause.

While Granny would skip, some of the neighbor kids would join her. They couldn't understand how someone as old as Granny could still skip.

As Granny strolled down the street, she took notice of the cracks in the sidewalk, reciting to herself the old childhood ditty, "Step on a crack you break your mothers back." Some of the sidewalks in Fuchsia were old and crumbly. No one seemed to care. Everyone was more careful when they walked. Fuchsia natives didn't worry about little things like crumbly sidewalks. The little pebbles from the sidewalks made great skipping stones at the town pond.

Granny rounded the corner onto Main Street. Granny loved the quaint sight of the buildings on the Main Street of Fuchsia. Like the brightness of the town's name, the buildings on Main Street had a uniqueness all their own. Where other cities were bowing to conformity,

Fuchsia valued creativity when it came to their businesses and the buildings that housed those businesses. No siree, you wouldn't find those boring metal awnings and windows put in older buildings that didn't belong in older buildings. People in Fuchsia didn't care if Main Street had round, curved or large windows. They did care if a large window was made smaller by boards and other contraption things that ruined the uniqueness and quality of the building.

Fuchsia didn't have any ordinances against purple buildings, pink buildings or other bright colored structures. Fuchsia was a little too large to call itself a village, but it bordered on being too unique to make it a normal, encyclopedia-defined town. The stores on main street mirrored the uniqueness of the owners of the buildings and the names of the businesses mirrored the uniqueness of the shops themselves. It had always been that way in Fuchsia.

When new construction was added to Main Street and the downtown, it was understood that those new businesses had to add to the ambiance of the street and not be boring, run of the mill, buildings. For the most part, over the years the new merchants complied except for Jasper Diggs. He built a plain old building and painted it white, with plain old windows. He was in the doghouse with the Mayor, the city council and the people of Fuchsia, They ignored his business as if it had the plague. Finally, he gave in and since his business is a dog grooming and pet food and toy store, he remodeled and now the building presents itself as an upscale doghouse decorated with doggy treats. His business has never been better. Jasper got so into the trend that he sports a dog biscuit bow tie that he wears to work every day and the women who work in his store wear doggie treat earrings that they now make and sell

A few years ago, some hotty-tott manager came in and told the town they needed to hire someone to help them get it together. So they did. They hired Mr. Hotty Tot or as Granny thought of him, Mr. Hot Shot. He tried to tell Pickles Grocery that they had to take the huge lighted pickle on the roof of the grocery store down.

"That Pickle is an eyesore. No respectable town that wants to attract businesses and tourists should have a Pickle on top of a building. It must violate some code."

Then Mr. Hotty Tot, Hot Shot, told Nails Hardware Store that they had to remove the large Wrench Bench that they had in front of the store.

Mr. Nails had put a lot of sweat and tears into making his Wrench Bench. It was made out of the finest wrenches, welded together to make a sturdy bench that would hold the heftiest person. Mr. Nails got tired of having to repair his old bench after Godfrey and Annabelle Portowsky always sat on his bench and broke it because of their ample size

"The Wrench Bench is a danger to all. It's a hazard," Mr. Hotty Tott announced as he put his own hand into the wrenches on the side that were used as a railing. "This bench violates Fuchsia City Code 900210052," he yelled as his hand got stuck in the wrench, "Remove it immediately!"

His last mistake was deciding to fix the sidewalks. People were upset that they wouldn't have the stones to skip on the lake anymore. They would have had to find a different place for their supply. Well Mr. Hotty Tot, Hot Shot got put on ice one winter and got slid out of town.

Horatio Helicourt, the mayor of the fine community of Fuchsia and the city council, all twelve of them, held a special town meeting in light of Mr. Hotty Tot's departure.

"We will no longer fill the position of City Manager for the community of Fuchsia. We must protect our potholes. We must protect our signs and our benches. We must protect our Fuchsianess. I, Horatio Helicourt, along with the city council of Fuchsia, Minnesota, declare today, "Mr. Hotty Tott no more day. It will be celebrated on this day each year to remind us that Fuchsia, Minnesota, will not conform. Fuchsia, Minnesota, will march to their own drummer. Vote for me Horatio Helicourt at the next election, to keep your Fuchsianess."

Granny shook off the reminiscing and the memories and made a bee line for AbStract. AbStract was one of the biggest department stores in Granny's town of Fuchsia, Minnesota. It was known to carry the finest of everything for men and women. If you wanted a brass ring, you could fine it in AbStract. If you wanted a purse made out of candy wrappers, you could find it at Abstract. If you wanted glittery sky scraper shoes, you could find it at AbStract. The more money you had to spend, Abstract could help you spend it. For a town the size of Fuchsia, Abstract carried some of the finest and most unusual goods in Minnesota.

Granny took the time after stepping into the store to muss up her hair a little, make sure her stockings were still falling down and get into her shopper pose. She readied her umbrella and started to shop. What the residents and visitors to Fuchsia didn't know was that the merchants of Fuchsia had hired Granny as a Secret Security Officer to protect their goods.

Granny didn't actually make the arrests. People thought she was just an old disheveled lady who clumsily happened to get in the way of those who tried to steal from the merchants of Fuchsia. Granny liked keeping her job secret because she didn't want her kids and grandkids to know about it. They wouldn't like it and they would send her to the wrinkle farm. Her kids would declare, "Mom, catching crooks is too dangerous. You're going to get hurt. You're too old to be doing that." Granny figured hurt was better than dead and sitting around doing nothing made her feel dead. If she became dead while hooking a crook with her umbrella, her tombstone could read: Here lies Granny, she hooked a crook. That's better than reading a book.

Every day, Granny made the rounds of all the stores in Fuchsia. The clerks didn't know what Granny was up to. They thought she was a lonely old woman with nothing else to do but shop. Occasionally, she would buy something to throw everyone off the scent, but mostly she spent her time meandering around and occasionally engaging in conversation with other shoppers.

Granny carried a remote, quiet alarm in her pocket and when she saw a thief, she would pop the remote alarm and the Big Guy would come a running. If the thief was getting away, Granny used her umbrella to trip them or hit them over the head. Granny would then apologize profusely for being so clumsy. It slowed the thief down enough for the Big Guy to get there. They would arrest the thief and give a wink at Granny.

It always gave Granny a thrill to get in on something so exciting. Granny had dreamed of becoming a detective in her younger days but women didn't do that in her day. When she would bring it up to her family and friends, they would laugh at her. Every time she brought a crook down with her umbrella, she strutted a little prouder with her 5 foot, 100 lb frame. Old age had its benefits. She always looked harmless but she packed quite a punch.

Granny peeked out the front window of AbStract to see if there was any sign of her Corvette. Maybe her kids had taken it so she couldn't drive. Somewhere in her foggy memory she seemed to recall that there had been talk of not letting her drive anymore and taking her car away. Granny thought that would be something she would remember if they actually had taken it out of her garage. Granny didn't have time to worry about her car now. She had work to do. She saw her first target, um customer ahead of her.

Chapter Three

As Granny walked around AbStract, she didn't see anything unusual. Her target customer was a confused man trying to buy his wife some perfume. Granny lingered at the jewelry counter, fingered some lingerie in the lingerie department, had her usual cup of coffee in the AbStract coffee corner and decided to move on down the street.

"Hey Granny, what are you doing walking today? Where's that fancy car of yours?" Ditty Belle yelled to Granny from across the street.

"Just decided to get some exercise, Ditty," Granny replied. Granny secretly thought that Ditty, who owned the Persnickety Bookstore in Fuchsia, was coveting her car. Granny looked around to see if her car was anywhere to be seen, not wanting to admit she that she had lost it. Maybe Ditty took it. Granny wouldn't put it past her. One time Ditty couldn't find her roller skates so she borrowed Abe Felts' skates. The only problem was that she didn't ask and didn't tell. Abe was madder than a wet hen. Of course that was fifty years ago, but leopards don't change their spots.

Granny turned into Pickles Grocery store. She started walking the aisles. The fruit looked good today. The smell from the deli was making Granny's mouth water. She turned the corner by the canned gourmet shrimp and tuna. She narrowed her eyes. Yup, there was shrimp being poached. Cans were going into hidden pockets.

Granny sauntered up to the beady-eyed man. Innocently, she took her umbrella crook and tried to reach something on the top shelf above the man's head. She had him blocked so he couldn't move. She pushed the button in her pocket to alert the Big Guy and then with the snap of her umbrella hook she brought all the cans from the top shelf down on the head of the beady-eyed man.

Granny was quick; she jumped back to avoid the cans as they crashed. Then Granny started apologizing profusely to the beady-eyed man.

"I'm sorry, I am so sorry. Are you hurt? Let me help you." And with that, Granny pretended to accidently drop the umbrella on his head.

"Are you an idiot?" The beady-eyed man yelled at her as he tried to extricate himself from the cans.

Granny immediately, accidently on purpose, caught his ankle in the crook of her umbrella and he went tumbling back down.

Just as the man let out a bellow, "Leave me alone! You're a disaster!" the Big Guy came swooping down and hauled him away, again winking at Granny so no one else would see.

Granny straightened her disheveled clothes, pushed down her stockings some more and was ready to proceed to the next store. Granny turned around to find someone watching her. Granny felt almost as if she were looking at herself in the mirror. The old woman who looked back at her could have almost been her clone except for the red hair sticking out from underneath her hat. It had to be a dye job. Granny's hair was bright gray. Granny's was a dye job too but bright gray looked better than washed out gray. Red was another story altogether.

Granny made her way over to the woman. This woman was dressed similar to Granny. Her stockings were wrinkled and pulled down closer to her ankles. Her clothes were disheveled and torn in places. Instead of an umbrella, this woman carried a cane and walked with a limp.

"Hello, I'm Gram Gramstead," the lady said as she introduced herself to Granny. "Are you alright? I couldn't help but notice that terrible accident. And the man was a crook; you could have been hurt."

"All I was doing was trying to get a can of shrimp from the top shelf and the cans tumbled down. I didn't know that the man was a crook," Granny exclaimed. "I was so scared. I was trembling and then I hit that poor man. When they hauled him away because he was a crook, I almost fainted from fear. This is too much excitement for an old woman." Granny sat down on the floor feigning faintness.

The red haired old woman quickly limped to the water fountain in the corner, grabbed a cup, filled it with water, ran back over and threw it in Granny's face.

"Oh, oh, does that feel better?" the red haired Gram Gramstead fussed worriedly over Granny.

"Was that necessary?" Granny held in her temper, as she wiped her face with her hat. After all, the red haired woman didn't know about her undercover work.

"You were fainting; I couldn't think of anything else to do," Gram Gramstead exclaimed as she helped Granny to her feet.

Granny, who was still pretending to be weak so she wouldn't blow her cover and still trying to reign in her temper, got to her feet and wobbled down the aisle. "Then thank you, dear. I must be going."

Gram Gramstead walked beside her. "I hope we meet again and I hope you get over your awful scare." With that, the red headed Gram walked out the door of Pickles. Granny watched with an open mouth as Gram Gramstead got into a red 1957 Corvette in the parking lot, squealed her tires and roared away.

Granny continued her sleuthing, stopping at Rack's Restaurant, Nail's Hardware, Red Lulu's Quilt Shop, Headache's Drug Store, and The Ecstatic Emporium, ending her day, at Ella's Enchanted Forest. It was a quiet day after Pickles Grocery. The only puzzling event of the day was a well dressed, good looking young man who seemed to be at every store Granny visited. It wasn't unusual for visitors to Fuchsia to do the tourist thing and visit the stores, so it wasn't strange to see this man in every store. She watched him carefully and his pockets didn't seem to be getting any fuller. He didn't touch anything. He would look, but not touch. He didn't buy anything either. Maybe he was killing time waiting for his wife to finish her shopping in another store.

What puzzled Granny about this young man was the fact that he was always in a store when she left and by the time she got to her new destination, he was already there. He hadn't passed her on the street. There wasn't a faster alternative route. But he was always there ahead of her.

Granny started home on foot not having found her car. As she walked, she wondered about the coincidence of the red haired old lady named Gram Gramstead having the same identical car as she did. Maybe she had a twin her parents hadn't told her about 70 years ago.

Granny turned into her driveway and noticed her garage door ajar. When she looked in, her car was sitting right where it was supposed to be. Maybe she imagined it wasn't there this morning. Maybe she didn't even check. She couldn't remember.

Fish was waiting for her as she opened the door to her house. Granny wondered what precious present he had brought her today when she heard a yap. Granny turned and found Fish sitting next to a miniature white poodle, wagging his tail. Fish looked like the cat that swallowed the canary and was presenting it to his master. The poodle nudged Fish as if she were in love. Granny could see she had a situation.

Chapter Four

"Fish, where did you get that poodle? Take her back this instant." Fish just yawned while Granny scolded. When did a cat respond to a command? Granny reached down to pick up the poodle when Fish did something he'd never done before. He hissed at Granny. Granny drew back in amazement.

"What was that, Fish? I haven't heard you hiss since the pet store. You are a feisty cutie."

Fish looked at Granny, nudged the white poodle and proceeded to take the poodle in every room of the house to show her around before crawling under the bed with her to go to sleep.

Granny rolled her eyes and headed to the refrigerator to get a big bowl of ice cream for dinner when there was a knock on the door. Granny started to the door, but the visitor opened the door and was in the room before Granny could take a step.

"Mom, Mom, where are you?" Penelope saw Granny standing in the kitchen and prattled on before Granny could answer. "Where have you been? Are you ok? I've been trying to call you all day. I had to drive all this way to check on you to make sure you weren't laying on the floor somewhere gasping your last breath."

"As you see, Penelope, I'm just fine." Penelope was Granny's oldest daughter and lived thirty miles away in Allure, Minnesota. "I was out and about."

"You didn't drive, did you?" Penelope asked

"No, of course I didn't drive." She didn't tell Penelope that the reason she didn't drive was that she couldn't find her car. Or the fact that maybe she imagined she couldn't find her car and it had been in the garage all day.

Penelope walked over to the refrigerator and opened it, peering inside. "Mom, you have no food. I'll take you out to dinner and then we'll go grocery shopping. All you have in the fridge and freezer are ice cream and donuts."

Penelope took Granny's arm, handed Granny the umbrella and escorted her out the door to the car. Granny knew better than to protest. It was easier to go with the flow when Penelope was in this mood. Besides, it might be a change to have something other than ice cream for dinner. Granny loved her ice cream but she could make an exception for one night if it made Penelope happy.

"I'll drive," Granny spit out as she pulled her arm out of Penelope's grasp and headed for her garage.

"You most certainly will not. The last time I drove with you, we ended up in someone's rose bush with one of the branches wrapped around my neck like a necklace. I don't want to repeat that thorny situation." With that, Penelope grabbed Granny's arm, led her across the lawn and plunked her in the passenger seat of Penelope's Honda Civic.

Granny never being one not to have the last word, stated, "Be sure to put on your seatbelt, Penelope. We don't fix potholes in Fuchsia. We use potholes instead of rumble strips to slow people down. If I were driving, I'd know where each and every one is." Granny warned Penelope, "I was trying to save you and your car, but since you won't let me drive I can't help you. Don't blame me when your car falls through a pothole and we have to have the Fuchsia Rescue Squad rescue us. Don't say I didn't warn you." Granny shook her finger as a warning to Penelope and then quickly fastened her seatbelt, clamped her mouth shut and didn't open it again until they reached the parking lot at their destination.

Penelope drove into Rack Restaurant's parking lot, parked the car and led Granny straight to a booth in the back of the restaurant. Granny was happy with the seating arrangement. She could watch everyone in the restaurant. She might as well work her undercover job as long as she was here. Rack's only paid her for day work but she'd throw this in for free. Granny smiled to herself, knowing Penelope had no idea she was helping Granny with her work.

When Penelope and Granny had settled into the booth, Penelope grabbed Granny's hand and patted it. "Mom, see we made it here in one piece. No potholes, no rose bush fatalities and I was able to park under that nice tree outside close to the door in spite of your protests that the tree would come to life while we were in here and eat my car."

Granny patted Penelope's hand and replied in a meek and mild voice, "Well, maybe I exaggerate a little bit, but what does an old lady like me have to do?" Granny lowered her eyes, gave Penelope a sad look and continued on, "I guess you know best, dear, after all I am old and feeble and my memory just isn't what it used to be. I must have been thinking about a tree in some fairy tale."

Penelope gave Granny a sympathetic look and opened her menu. Granny kept her head lowered afraid she might give the glee she felt inside of herself away. Penelope didn't know there was a real reason Granny had warned her not to park under the tree. Every resident in Fuchsia knew not to park under the tree at night. The tree was some sort of weird weeping willow. At night it would weep even more and envelope anything that was under it in its branches and hold on tight until the morning light when it would again open its branches. Penelope wouldn't be able to say Granny didn't warn her. After all, what does a forgetful old woman know? Once Granny got her smile under control, she picked up her menu.

Penelope ordered broiled walleye for Granny along with a lettuce salad, broccoli, and milk, to help Granny's bones, or so Penelope said. "You have to drink milk, mom, you need to keep those bones strong."

Granny rolled her eyes when Penelope wasn't looking. She knew Penelope meant well. Granny slyly looked around and watched all the customers out of the corners of her eyes so Penelope wouldn't suspect what she was doing. Granny took her eyes off of the other diners for a minute to glance out the window next to the booth. She blinked her eyes. She couldn't be seeing what she thought she saw. It was that red haired old woman, driving a red corvette, waving at her. Granny closed her eyes for a second and glanced again. This time, all Granny saw, was Mrs. Periwinkle feeding her squirrels across the street. Granny decided that her foggy memory now must be fogging her eyes.

As Penelope left to use the ladies room, Granny winked at an older man in the second booth across the restaurant. She liked to wink at handsome men around her age. You never knew who you might meet and at her age she couldn't wait around for them to make the first move. She smiled as he winked back. Glancing over at the tables, Granny saw trouble. A thirty something woman was slyly brushing past tables of diners who had recently left and left their tips and payment for dinner on the tables. Granny could see as the woman passed the tables the tips and payments were being brushed into her purse. Granny had to act fast. She pushed the remote button in her pocket to alert the Big Guy. Granny was never without her remote when she was out on the town. Granny grabbed the glasses of water on her table, snagged her umbrella, and proceeded to weave down the restaurant knocking into the woman, spilling both glasses of water over the woman's head and securing the woman's ankle with the crook of her umbrella.

"I'm sorry. I am so sorry." Granny proclaimed loudly for the whole restaurant to hear. Then Granny reached over to pretend to try and help the woman up and instead she fell on her. Again Granny proclaimed, "I'm so sorry. I'm so clumsy." As Granny was straightening up and the woman was ready to let Granny have it, the Big Guy swooped in and took the woman away. The Big Guy winked at Granny so she'd know she did a great job.

Loud applause broke out as The Big Guy left the building with the woman. Granny, turned around and pretended to ignore the applause as she hobbled back to join Penelope.

"Mom, mom, what are you doing? Are you ok? Why did you run into that woman? Were you lightheaded? Do we need to take you to the doctor?" Penelope was agitated.

Granny patted her arm and said, "I just felt a little weak; it must be from not eating well all week. I went to the other table to ask the waiter for more water. Our glasses seemed to be empty." Granny lifted her glasses to show Penelope the empty glass.

Granny and Penelope finished their meal. While they were paying their bill, Granny glanced over to the far corner and there sat the good looking young man she'd seen earlier in the day at the stores. He seemed to be watching her.

Granny was a little disappointed that it wasn't dark enough when they left Racks for the tree to have weeped over Penelope's car.

"See, mom, nothing happened to my car. We really need to do something about your anxiety. Perhaps we should make you an appointment with Dr. Armhammer."

"That quack? He's a hack," Granny chuckled to herself at that sentence; maybe she took after her mother in the rhyming department after all. "Last time I visited Dr. Armhammer, I had to put a hammer hold on him, thought he was going to give me one of them shots for the flu.

Well, flu who to him. I guess he found out what it was to be stuck, with his own needle, that is. It took two receptionists and a little five year old patient to calm him down. Just thought he should get a little of his own medicine so he knew what it felt like. Strange thing, they won't take my calls anymore," Granny announced with satisfaction.

Penelope kept her eyes on the road and took a firm grip on the steering wheel, concentrating on their destination. She didn't want to be accused of murdering an old woman in broad daylight who happened to be her mother. What had happened to the proper woman who had raised her? Who was this woman? Penelope definitely had to take this up with her siblings.

They stopped at Pickles Grocery and Penelope bought Granny, milk, soy milk, yogurt, Acai juice, organic eggs, fresh fruit, fresh vegetables and fish. Granny knew it would do no good to protest. Fish would love all this food. He happened to have an appetite to eat healthy human food. Granny would make a trip tomorrow when she was working undercover for her ice cream and donuts.

While Penelope was checking out, Granny felt someone watching her. It was a prickle up her backside. She turned slowly and looked out of the corner of her eyes. It was strange because it was the same young man from Rack's who was now at Pickles. How could that be? He was at the restaurant when they left and they drove straight to Pickles and now he was here ahead of them?

Granny was about to march over to confront him when she heard the checkout clerk speaking in a loud voice, "Granny did you want your usual…?" Granny didn't let her finish the sentence.

"No, I don't want my usual exlax. I have enough at home," stopping the clerk from giving her the usual Ambrosia wine that she kept in stock for Granny. Granny grabbed Penelope's arm and said loudly for everyone to hear, "I must go, I must go, I have enough for the night. I'm worn out. It's too much for me to be out this late, Penelope. Help me to the car." With a wink at the clerk, Granny hobbled outside.

Penelope dropped Granny at home and insisted on tucking her into bed. Granny donned her Granny pajamas, kissed Penelope good night and thanked her for her help.

"And mom," Penelope instructed, "no more flip flops." Penelope grabbed the flip flops sitting by the bed and took them with her as she walked out the door.

Granny watched through the break in her blinds as Penelope drove away. Granny waited a good five minutes before she got back out of bed in case Penelope forgot something. The first thing Granny did was get another pair of flip flops out of the pillow case that covered Fish's cat bed in the corner of the room. Granny kept them stashed there just for a flip flop emergency like tonight.

Granny leaned under the bed. "Fish, you can come out now. Bring your friend; you can keep her." For some reason, Fish seemed to understand that. Fish and the little white poodle crawled out from underneath the bed and followed Granny into the living room.

Granny dug out her binoculars and checked to see if the boxer shorts were off the pole. They were. George was safe. Granny then checked on Sally. Her shade was down. She was in for the night. Granny peered into Mavis' window. The lights were blazing and Mavis was having an imaginary conversation with someone, gesturing wildly. Mavis then waved at Granny, plopped down on the couch and turned the light off. Everyone was tucked in for the night. Granny locked the door and changed from her granny gown into her hot pink, shortie nightgown, crawled into bed and turned off the light. She heard the wisp of the pet door as Fish and his new poodle friend went out for the night.

Granny sighed "I wonder what tomorrow will bring."

Chapter Five

The ring of the phone woke Granny out of a deep sleep. She'd been dreaming about the handsome older man that she had winked at in the restaurant. Granny grabbed the phone. "This better be good to wake me up," Granny shouted into the phone.

"Granny, there's something happening downtown," Mrs. Shrill from the next block yelled into Granny's ear. "Baskerville started howling and woke me up. I peeked out of the window and saw police cars and an ambulance heading toward town. Baskerville just keeps howling. Do you know what's happening?"

"How would I know what's happening? You just woke me up," Granny shouted back into the phone.

Mrs. Shrill replied, "You go downtown every morning. You're in the know."

"Since the only time you've ever talked to me was to "tut, tut, tut" me, I wouldn't tell you if I knew." And with those words, Granny slammed the phone down on the stand.

Granny picked up her cell phone, also by her bed, to see if she'd gotten any calls. She usually turned her cell phone off during the night. The only people who ever called her cell phone were the merchants she worked for in her undercover job. Nope, no calls.

Granny hurried to get dressed in her disheveled clothes, quickly got her binoculars and checked on her neighbors, fed Fish and the little white poodle and rushed out the door. Hopefully, her car would be in the garage this morning.

Granny gave a huge whoop when she saw that her car was where it was supposed to be. She hopped into the red Corvette and tore out of her garage heading toward Main Street.

Granny couldn't believe her eyes when she pulled up down the block from AbStract. There were more police milling around the street than she knew they had in Fuchsia. An ambulance was also sitting running in front of the store. Granny grabbed her umbrella and headed for the Big Guy who was meticulously studying the building.

Granny dropped her umbrella next to the Big Guy so they could have a conversation without anyone being suspicious.

"What's happening?" Granny whispered.

"Someone broke into AbStract and stole all the jewelry from the jewelry cases. The alarm was turned off and no doors or windows had been pried open. There's no evidence of a break in. It has to be someone with a key. I'm adding to your duties. I want you to watch all the clerks and employees today too for any suspicious behavior. They're used to you browsing but they don't know why you're browsing."

"Why the ambulance?"

"When Jack Puffleman got to work and noticed the jewelry all gone, he called 911 and then fainted. He claims he didn't faint but had a whiff of some perfume and then things started to get fuzzy. My opinion: he fainted and doesn't want to admit it."

Granny shook her head, loudly thanked the Big Guy for helping her pick up her umbrella, and proceeded on down the street to start her day at another store until all the hoopla settled down at AbStract.

The Big Guy, as Granny had dubbed him, watched Granny slowly make her way down the street. He thought he saw her take a skip and a hop as he turned his head back to business at hand at Abstract. Cornelius Ephram Stricknine, his given name at birth, wondered if he had made a bad decision when he had relocated to the quaint town of Fuchsia, Minnesota, to become their lead detective/police chief. Everyone called him "the Big Guy" because of his large, hulking stature. Cornelius preferred it that way since his real name always seemed to evoke loud guffaws or people choking from trying to hold back their laughter at his unusual name. He couldn't count the strychnine jokes he had endured.

Preparing to go back into Abstract to investigate the crime brought back memories from his past career that he didn't want to relive. It wasn't something he was proud of and he didn't want to repeat his past mistakes here.

As he contemplated the task at hand, he hoped this was just an ordinary run of the mill burglary. Fuchsia had seemed to be the perfect, quiet, town to move to. He'd been told it was low on crime, people minded their own business and that it was a neat, orderly town. He was beginning to wonder if he'd been sold a bag of goods, especially when it came to people minding their own business.

Then there was Granny. She was a little strange. He didn't quite know what to make of her but she seemed to be part of the package of this job in Fuchsia. Who had ever heard of an undercover Granny?

Chapter Six

Granny's first stop was at Ella's Enchanted Forest. The owner, Delight Delure, greeted Granny as she walked in the door.

"Did you see anything strange yesterday at AbStract?" Since Delight knew who Granny was because she also was one of Granny's customers, Granny felt comfortable talking to her about the heist.

"Not a thing. The only thing I noticed was this tourist, cute young man. I wish I were forty years younger. I'd have winked at him."

Delight remarked, "I'm glad I don't have anything quite as exciting as diamonds to steal. My shop should be pretty safe from burglars unless they're hungry and like plants." Ella's Enchanted Forest sold tasty chocolates, baked treats to die for, gourmet coffee and unusual plants, trees and floral items. It was "enchanted" because of the goodies to eat and "forest" because of the huge array of greenery and trees that made her shop look like a forest. Her forest room had a retractable roof for the trees to grow tall.

The conversation ended when customers started pouring into the Enchanted Forest. Granny stuffed a cream puff into her mouth and started meandering around. As she stopped to examine a pin lying on the floor next to a plant, Granny looked up to see the same young man from yesterday watching her. She picked up the pin, straightened up and decided to confront the young man. The only problem was that when she looked up, he was gone. Had she imagined she saw him? Was her fogginess starting to affect her so she was imagining things?

Granny continued her rounds at the stores, ready to end her day at AbStract. All the hoopla should have settled down now so she could easily observe all the customers. As she walked out of Headache's Drugstore she thought she saw the red haired old woman Gram Gramstead cruising down the street in the red Corvette. Granny glanced over to where she had parked her own car; it was still there.

As Granny entered AbStract, she noticed the detectives from Fuchsia's Police Department still there. She walked over to the almost empty jewelry case. Justine a girl from another department came to help her. "Can I help you, Granny? We had a little problem today so we don't have much to show you. Those long, dangly, purple and pink, junkyard earrings that you admired the other day were part of what was stolen."

"That's ok, dear. You know mostly I just look. Someone my age and weak like me just wants to grab looks at what we used to be able to wear. Where's Estelle who usually works this counter?" Granny asked.

"We don't know. She didn't come to work. They can't find her. They think she might have had something to do with the jewelry heist. They found an earring she was wearing yesterday behind the counter. She could have lost it when she was working, but she was last seen here. It was her night to close and lock up the store."

Granny shook her head and turned away from the counter and looked straight into the face of the cute young man who always seemed to be watching her. Granny started over to confront him but all of sudden he was gone.

Granny turned to Justine, "Justine, do you know that young man who was lurking over there in the corner?"

"Ah, no." Justine looked at Granny with a puzzled expression. "I've never seen anyone lurking in that corner, ever! There's nothing there, and if there was a good looking young man anywhere in the store, I'd have noticed! More importantly, he would have noticed me." Justine shook her long blonde hair, batted her eyes at Granny, gave Granny the look and continued, "After all, who could resist my come hitherness?" Justine flashed a come hither look at Granny, turned away and admired herself in the mirror.

Granny shook her head in amusement at Justine's confidence and turned around to take another look, but the good looking young man seemed to have disappeared into thin air. As she started walking out of AbStract deep in thought, she tripped over her own umbrella and started to tumble to the ground. A pair of strong arms caught her from falling. She looked up to see who had rescued her and looked straight into the face of the handsome older man who she had winked at in Rack's Restaurant the previous night. She quickly wondered if she pretended a faint, if it would buy her a little more time in his arms. You were never too old to imagine romance.

"Are you all right, young lady?" The man asked and then he winked at her. Granny flustered, blushed and answered in a quiet voice. "I am now."

"It's been awhile since I had someone fall into my arms."

Granny blushed again and answered, "It's been awhile since I fell for someone." Granny gave a wink and walked out the door. Granny stopped once she was clear of the door and checked herself out. She was trembling from head to foot and not with fear but with little prickles of excitement in her heart. That was unusual because Granny wasn't prone to swooning.

Granny walked to her car. She could swear she had left the top up, but now it was down, showing the beautiful red interior of her car. Granny hopped in and squealed out of her parking stall, checking first to see that the eagle eyes of the patrolman weren't watching her.

Granny pulled into her garage, waving at George, Sally, and Mavis who were out on Mavis' lawn having an animated discussion. Mavis must have talked them into joining her imaginary reality show. As Granny walked into her house, she greeted Fish and the little white poodle that was still following Fish around as if she were in love. Granny reached down to see what little present Fish had brought her today. At least it wasn't another poodle. Granny took a minute to wonder who the poodle belonged to before she gazed at the object she had picked up. She couldn't believe her eyes. It was a long, dangly, purple and pink Junkyard earring just like the ones she had admired in AbStract.

Granny held the earring in her hand, felt the unique roughness of the jewels and the rusted steel, and wondered if perhaps she actually had put the earring in her pocketbook in her fogginess. Perhaps Fish had been in her pocketbook again and stole it from her. Perhaps the jewel thieves had not taken this pair of earrings but she had.

"Where did you get this? Where did you get this?" Granny yelled in agitation showing the earring to the lop-eared cat.

"Meow!" Fish gave her what seemed like a crooked grin, meowed a little louder, nudged the little white poodle and promptly rolled over on the floor and started purring at her feet.

Granny quickly picked up her pocketbook and dumped out the contents. No, the other earring wasn't there. Granny wasn't sure what to make of this. The little white poodle was jumping for attention. Granny noticed he had something dangling from his mouth and was trying to give it to her. She reached down and took it from his mouth. It was another earring but it wasn't one of Granny's and Granny had never seen it before. The little white poodle, proud of himself for having a present for Granny too, sidled up to Fish and nuzzled his nose, and playfully plopped down right on top of Fish.

Granny patted their heads, headed to the refrigerator and took out her ice cream and donuts for her dinner. She put the rest of the vegetables, the fruit and the yogurt that Penelope had brought her in Fish and the little white poodle's bowl. After all she had to keep her pets healthy.

Granny was glad tomorrow was Saturday. It had been a puzzling week. A weekend of rest and relaxation was just what she needed to rejuvenate for the next week.

After dinner, Granny visited her exercise room in the basement. While she lifted weights, Fish walked on the treadmill. The cat seemed to be in another world pretending he was hunting prey while he was on Granny's treadmill. Little white poodle investigated the exercise ball and kept trying to crawl on top of it. She would bark with excitement when the exercise ball would hit her nose and try to roll over her.

After checking on her neighbors with her binoculars, Granny crawled into bed wearing her purple leather PJs and promptly fell asleep to the sound of the pet door swishing as Fish and little white poodle went out for the night.

Chapter Seven

Granny woke to the sun shining in her eyes. She had slept late. It was almost 7:00 a.m. It was Saturday so Granny pulled out a box of chocolates and settled down to read in bed for a while. She was deeply entranced with her new novel *Fifty Shades of Grey* by E.L. James, when she heard her front door open.

"Mom, Mom where are you? We're all here. Mom?" Then Granny heard more door banging and more footsteps.

Granny quickly hid the chocolates under the bed, stuck her book in between the mattress, and pulled up the covers so her purple leather PJ's could not be seen, just as her bedroom door opened. Penelope, Starshine and Thor walked into the room. Starshine and Thor were Granny's second and third born children.

"Mom, what are you doing still in bed?" Penelope asked.

Thor looked at her concerned. "Aren't you feeling well?"

"Can you not get out of bed?" Starshine whispered afraid.

"I'm fine, just a little tired after my hard week of watching television. Those programs wear you out more than you know," Granny replied. "What time is it?"

Penelope replied, "It's 10 o'clock."

Wow, the time sure passed quickly from 7:00 a.m. She was so engrossed in her book and her chocolates she had forgotten to get out of bed to check on the neighbors. "What are you all doing here?" Granny thought to ask.

"We're going to clean your house. Thor is going to work on the outside and Starshine and I are going to work on the inside."

Granny looked at Penelope and said, "I think I'll rest in bed while all the hoopla of cleaning is going on. I don't know if I can take that much excitement." Granny gazed at them with a feigned tired look.

"You rest, mom; let us take care of you. That's our job now. You took care of us, so we need to help you." Starshine answered with a soft voice.

Penelope continued on where Starshine had left off. "Mom, we know you're getting up there in age and things are getting difficult. We want you to think about moving in with us. We'll talk about that on another day. Just think about it." She left the room, not seeing Granny's look of horror.

Thor was the last to leave the room. "Ok, lock the door; hide the chocolates and whatever book you're reading that will shock your daughters. I only came along to see that my sisters don't get carried away. And I'll tune up your car but we'll let them think I'm disabling it so you can't drive."

Thor winked at Granny and walked out of the room.

Thor was a good boy. He was the youngest and had been the hardest to raise. Her late husband Ferdinand Fiddlestadt's last words on his deathbed had been about Thor.

"Don't cut him any slack, Hermiony; he's just like you, crazy and out of control. It took a firm hand like mine to keep you in control and now you have to take over and use a firm hand with Thor," Ferdinand Fiddlestadt raised his head, raised his arms and muttered, "God help her." And he breathed his last breath.

Hermiony, who had kept all the impishness hidden inside of herself for a long time, realized she didn't have her momma or daddy or Ferdinand to remind her of how a proper lady should act. For a brief instant Hermiony's face broke out in a mischievous smile. Hermiony sat quietly for a moment and then snuck over to her closet, turned around to make sure Ferdinand was really in a higher place and upended a loose floorboard. Hermiony started to open the floor board but quickly thought twice. She grabbed a scarf and scurried back to Ferdinand's permanently sleeping body and draped the scarf gently over his face. 'Sorry, Ferdinand, sorry momma, sorry daddy; I hope you can't see me." Hermiony hesitated, bowed her head in a silent prayer and then ran back over to the loose floorboard and pulled out a tiny pink mini-skirt from underneath the floorboard. She'd kept it hidden for years, only taking it out to gaze at it longingly, knowing she could never wear it. Hermiony made sure the door was locked, checked Ferdinand's face to make sure it was covered and donned her pink mini-skirt. Hermiony savored the moment. She took a deep breath, closed her eyes and imagined she was out dancing and laughing and taking risks. Hermiony opened her eyes, whisked off the mini- skirt and donned her respectable, mother clothes, took the scarf off of Ferdinand's eyes, touched Ferdinand's cheek with a kiss and said, "I won't let you down." With that, Hermiony put on a somber face, opened the door and prepared to raise her girls and keep Thor under control on her own.

Granny snapped her thoughts back to the present day and quickly got out of the bed, grabbed her clothes and opened the trap door in the back of the closet built into the wall. She stashed her chocolates, her *Fifty Shades of Grey* book, her flashy night clothes and her manual on how to catch a crook when he doesn't want to be caught. She shoved the shoe rack over the secret door and proceeded to make her way to the living room to watch the progress of the house cleaning.

"Mom, why do you have four empty bowls on the floor?" Starshine asked.

Granny answered quickly with a meek face, "I was scrubbing the floor and I decided it would be easier for me to use small bowls of water."

Penelope put the bowls in the dishwasher. We need to close up that old pet door that's been here since you bought the house too. It's been a long time since our pets darkened your pet door. May Ooky and Booky rest in peace." Penelope put her hands over her heart while thinking about the twin beagles they used to own.

Thor, walking in and hearing the conversation, said "I'll do it another time; it's not going to hurt anything. No intruder could fit through that door and if I were a critter I wouldn't attempt to get one over on mom by trying to sneak into this house." Then he winked at Granny. Granny winked back.

Granny read a magazine and watched as her house was cleaned from top to bottom. Granny hoped Thor would buy the groceries to restock her refrigerator because he'd sneak in her candy and ice cream and donuts. After they all left with warnings that they'd be back in a couple of weeks, Granny pulled out the pet bowls, refilled them with food and water and headed for bed after checking on her neighbors. It had been a long day. Fish and the little white poodle hadn't been back but Granny wasn't worried. Fish knew enough to stay out of the way when her family was here or he might be thrown to the dogs at the pound. They would like a tasty cat.

Chapter Eight

Granny woke Sunday morning, checked on her neighbors, donned her best respectable Granny clothes, hopped into her red Corvette and headed to church. We Save You Christian Church was across town.

We Save You Christian Church was the only church in town. It catered to everyone—Lutherans, Presbyterians, Methodists and even Catholics. It didn't matter what denomination you were when you moved to Fuchsia, you ended up at We Save You Christian Church. Some weeks you got a Lutheran Service, some weeks you got a Methodist Service and some weeks the Priest from Allure popped over to do a Catholic Service. Some weeks you weren't sure what denomination you were practicing. It was always a surprise when you got to church. You never knew what you were gonna get, but you knew it was gonna be good. As long as you had faith, that was good enough for everyone in Fuchsia. Maybe the element of surprise was the reason the church was always so full, standing room only most Sundays.

Granny got there just in time to greet Preacher Hester Snicks and slide into the pew next to Tricky Travis Trawler.

Granny got her umbrella ready. She had this all planned out. Every Sunday, Tricky Travis tried to pilfer from the collection plate. Every Sunday, Granny found a way to stop him and this Sunday was no exception. He tried to crawl out of the pew when Granny sat down next to him, but Granny blocked his way with her umbrella. When he tried to crawl the other way she hooked his pants. If he would have continued crawling he would have been crawling without his pants. Since Travis didn't want to be noticed all he could do was quietly sit back down on the pew. When the collection plate was passed, you would think, because Travis knew Granny was watching, that he wouldn't try his pilfering, but common sense wasn't one of Travis' better known qualities. This Sunday when he reached his hand into the plate and came out with a handful of money, Granny put down the pointy end of her umbrella hard on the top of his foot. Travis rose up a good yardstick off of the pew and his hand instinctively unclenched and let go of the money.

Granny felt a tap on her shoulder and turned around. It was the red headed old woman, Gram Gramstead. "Good job, Granny; I couldn't have done it better myself." Gram got up, turned and walked out of the church.

Granny stared after her. This time Granny had got a good look at her face. There was something about her in between her wrinkles that looked familiar. Granny quickly put it out of her mind and concentrated on Pastor Snick's sermon.

As Granny was walking out of church, she looked up to see the same young man who she had seen in every store that she had been patrolling staring at her. Granny blinked and he was gone. Was he a figment of her imagination?

Granny tripped over her umbrella as she was trying to locate the young man. She started to fall head first into the crowd, when strong arms held her up. She looked up into the face of the handsome older man who she seemed to always fall for.

"Falling for me again; it seems it's getting to be a habit." The handsome man steadied her on her feet, winked at her and walked out the church door.

Granny straightened her clothes, tried to control her blush and followed him out the church door. Where was her car? She was sure she drove it to church.

Granny walked to the spot in the parking lot where she knew that she'd left her car. She turned in a full circle to see if she could spot her car. There weren't many cars left in the lot and a red Corvette would certainly stand out.

Pastor Snicks came out of the church and walked over to Granny. "Is there a problem, Granny?"

"No, no, I was just looking at the cracks in the cement. It seems we need to do something about this parking lot," Granny answered in a weak voice, wondering what he would say if he knew she'd lost her car.

"I'm sorry you had to park so far away. I was late getting to the service because of an emergency nursing home call. I noticed your car parked behind the church a couple of blocks away. We need to expand our parking lot. Do you want a lift to your car? That's one of the perks of being Pastor. They give you your own parking space."

Granny's face lit up. "I can walk. Actually that's why I left it there. Exercise is good for the soul. Don't you agree, Pastor?" With that, Granny took off at a fast sprint and then remembered she didn't want anyone to know she could walk so fast. She plunked the tip of her umbrella down on the ground, slowed down, used her umbrella for a cane and limped off.

When Granny saw her car, she raised her hands to thank the Lord. Except she didn't remember parking there and she was sure she'd left the top up on her car because it looked like rain. Maybe her kids were right. Maybe it was time for her to give up and move in with them. Granny shuddered at the thought and drove home.

When Granny walked in the door, a huge and furry something leapt into her arms and started licking her face. "What, aahh, no!" screamed Granny as she fended off the attack, finally getting the creature back on the floor. After Granny's heart quit pounding out of her chest, she looked down to see the biggest fur ball she'd ever seen sitting next to Fish and the little white poodle.

"Fish, you need to quit bringing home animals. I'm going to call animal control." Granny started to pull out her cell phone when Fish started meowing, the little white poodle started barking and the big fur ball started hissing. They were right. If Granny called animal control, her kids might find out she had Fish and Fish was here to stay if Granny had her way.

She'd have to hunt for the owners of these other creatures on her own. Granny looked closer at the big tan fur ball. She had blue eyes, was bigger than Fish, her ears had tips of black and so did her tail. Granny knew she was a she because Fish had an eye for the ladies and wouldn't have let a he cat in this house. But this creature was so round and so covered with long fur that it was hard to find her eyes in the midst of all that fluffy stuff. If you looked closely, you could see two little blue points staring out at you.

Granny had enough excitement for the day. She grabbed her ice cream and chocolates and headed to bed. Her neighbors would have to check on each other. A day in bed with a good book would do wonders for Granny's foggy memory.

Chapter Nine

Granny awoke the next morning to the phone blaring in her ear. "I'm sleeping!" Granny yelled to the unknown caller on the other end as she grabbed the phone.

"There's something happening downtown. Do you know what it is? Granny slammed the receiver down on Mrs. Shrill's shrill voice.

Granny peeked her big toe out of the blanket to see what kind of weather they were having today. Her big toe told her it could be a flip flop day. She squirmed and felt something sticky touch her hand. She must have fell asleep while eating her chocolates because she had just set her hand in melted chocolate on the sheets. Granny donned her flip flops, listened carefully to see if there was any unusual children noise in the house, and rousted herself out of bed.

She guessed she'd better make her way downtown and see what was happening. First she checked on her neighbors. They had made it through last night without her checking on them. George had got new boxer shorts to hang on the pole. These had red and purple stripes. Interesting.

Granny thought about her early morning phone call and a light bulb idea popped into her head. She skipped to the freezer and pulled out a package that said turkey bacon. She unwrapped the package and took out the Hormel Smoke Flavored bacon that she had hidden inside the turkey bacon package. Her kids always bought Granny turkey bacon. They meant well but she had made it to her age on whatever her taste buds told her to eat and she wasn't going to stop now. She didn't want the kids to feel bad so she let them think they were helping her while she still enjoyed the real stuff.

Granny fried up the bacon, singing a song while enjoying her latest plan. She tossed the fried bacon into a Ziploc bag, took out some tofu for the wild ones— Fish loved Tofu—and put her sparkly, high top tennis shoes on. She would walk down town past Mrs. Shrill's house.

Granny skipped down the street until she reached Mrs. Shrill's house. Baskerville was on the lawn waiting for her. Baskerville was only fed the best diet dog food they made. Occasionally Granny would slip him something tasty, like a piece of a hamburger, with Mrs. Shrill being none the wiser.

Granny took out her bag of bacon. She hollered "You hoo, Mrs. Shrill!" When Mrs. Shrill came to the door, Granny tossed all the bacon at Baskerville. She looked at Mrs. Shrill, pointed her finger and said "Tut, tut, tut!" Granny then took off in a fast sprint down the street, chuckling all the way to Main Street.

It was quite a scene that greeted Granny on Main Street. Police were milling all around Nail's Hardware Store. An ambulance was sitting outside just like at AbStract last week, but this time a fire truck was added to the scene. Mr. Nail was standing outside his building soaking wet. The Big Guy was examining the front door.

Granny pranced over to the Big Guy and accidently on purpose dropped her pocketbook. Dropping her umbrella again might have been too suspicious to onlookers. "What happened?"

"Another heist," Big Guy told Granny as he was helping her pick up the contents of her purse. "No locks broken, no alarm going off. Again it looks like an inside job."

"What happened to Mr. Nail?"

"He ran to his office to call 911 and while he was waiting for the police, he decided to have a smoke. He was so upset he threw the lit match into his wastebasket which started a fire, which set off the sprinklers, which doused the fire and Mr. Nail."

"I've got to get into the store before the crime scene is all cleaned up."

"One other thing you should know Granny, another clerk is missing. Her name is

Hermione. She was closing last night. All we found was one of her earrings. She didn't show up for work this morning and she doesn't answer her phone. We possibly have a gang with inside workers on these heists."

Big Guy finished handing Granny her purse and in a loud voice announced to Granny, "You can't go in there, Granny, it's a crime scene."

In a louder voice, Granny proclaimed, "You have to let me in. I have to use the ladies room. I'm old, my bladder will splatter. There's no time to run across the street."

"Ok, Granny, go straight to the ladies room, don't touch anything on the counter and don't step on any of the crime scene evidence left on the floor. Come right back out." He winked at Granny.

"My bladder will thank you," Granny said in a loud voice as she limped into the store on her umbrella.

Granny peeked around the shelves to make sure no one was watching her. All the police were outside interviewing possible witnesses. Granny studied the earring still left on the floor. Granny knew Hermione and it didn't look like an earring Hermione would wear. It was a long, beaded, red and purple dangly earring made out of nails. Hermione had commented once to Granny that she couldn't wear dangly earrings because she had a short neck.

Hermione and Granny had a little history although Hermione didn't know it. Granny and Hermione's dear, long departed mother had been best friends in Granny's young housewife years and since Hermione's mother had died, Granny had secretly kept an quiet eye on Hermione, sending money anonymously when she was in need. Once Granny also chased away a boyfriend who Granny knew was trouble. Hermione never did know why that rascal left town and left her high and dry and Granny never was going to reveal her part in his disappearance. Hermione's mom also had a little hidden mischievousness that Hermione had inherited and since Granny had the same spirit she knew her eagle eyes needed to be trained on Hermione as she was growing up. This was just another of Granny's secrets.

Granny stood up and glanced toward the back of the store. The good looking young man was standing in the back of the store by the saws and chains, glaring at Granny. How could that be? She was supposed to be the only one in here. Granny looked again and he was gone. She quickly ran to the back of the store and looked everywhere. The door to the back was blocked from the outside by the police. There was no other place he could have gone. Maybe she didn't see him. She would have to get her eyes checked, or her brain.

Granny walked out of the front door. "Thank you, thank you," Granny proclaimed in a loud voice. "You saved me." With that she winked at Big Guy, said in a low voice, "Later." and walked down the street to her next customer.

As Granny was proceeding to Red Lulu's Quilt Shop, she felt someone following her. When she turned around, there was the red haired old lady Gram Gramstead. "What are you doing following me?"

"I was trying to catch up with you. I thought we might have tea."

"Tea? I don't have tea. That's for little old ladies."

"Well, what do you think we are?" Gram answered back.

Granny gave her that look that dismissed Gram Gramstead and proceeded down the street.

Gram finally caught up with Granny again at Red Lulu's. "We have so much in common. We could be friends. I could help you."

"Help me do what?" Granny eyed her with a suspicious eye.

"Shop, isn't that what you do every day? I know what it's like to be lonely. I've been studying you. You are the ultimate shopper. You never buy anything except (Gram looked around to make sure no one was listening) wild lingerie."

"How do you know that? You've been spying on me."

"Isn't that young man peering at you from Lulu's front window good looking? Do you know him? He's been staring at you all the while we've been having this heart to heart chat."

Granny looked up to see the young man who she just saw in Nail's looking at her through the window from Lulu's. Who was he? At least now she knew he wasn't a figment of her imagination since this Gram Gramstead, stalker woman, saw him too. And how did he get to Lulu's so fast and why would he be in Lulu's since it was a quilt shop and men usually avoided anything to do with quilting.

"Gotta go. Oh, and by the way, we weren't having a heart to heart, I don't have one," Granny said to Gram as she pushed past Gram. Granny hurried into the store but the young man was gone. "Lulu, did you see where the young man who was just here disappeared to?"

"I'm sorry, Granny, I didn't see a young man. I was in the back of the store, but if he left through the front or back doors my ding dong bell would have sounded. Are you sure you saw him in here? Maybe it was just a reflection in the glass of someone standing beside you."

Granny looked through the front window and Gram Gramstead had disappeared too. There was something so familiar about her. Granny couldn't put her mind on it.

Granny finished checking Lulu's for sneaky shoppers, continued her rounds of the stores while pondering all the thefts and disappearances in Fuchsia the past week. This time they stole cat food, dog food and the big screen TV's that Nail's had recently started selling. Why would they steal cat food and dog food?

Granny walked home, passing Mrs. Shrill's house. Baskerville was not out so she couldn't toss him the steak she had picked up for him at Pickles. As she walked in her door, her phone was ringing.

"Granny, did you leave your car downtown? I noticed you walking home and I thought in all the excitement of my store being broken into that you might have forgotten that you drove to town," Mr. Nail inquired.

Granny's eyes grew wide with panic. She quickly replied, "I decided I needed a little exercise so I left it there. Your thoughtfulness is just too...too...I can't find the words. Yes, thoughtful, that's it." Granny thanked him again and with a puzzled look on her face, she walked out to her garage and found it empty. Granny felt something brush her leg. It was Furball. Furball dropped something at her feet. Granny picked it up. It was an earring that matched the earring that Big Guy claimed Hermione had been wearing the night before the heist.

Chapter Ten

Granny sank down to the concrete shaking her head. What was going on? Her car was gone. She was sure she didn't drive it to town. Animals kept turning up on her doorstep and they kept dropping earrings at her feet, not any earrings, but earrings that had been involved in a crime. Furball took that moment to interrupt her foggy train of thought by pouncing on her head and purring loudly. Granny flipped Furball off of her head, grabbed the edge of the garage door and slowly brought herself to her feet.

Granny hurried over to Mavis' house. "Mavis, Mavis, I need your help," Granny yelled as she knocked on Mavis door.

"Granny, I'm in here."

Granny walked into Mavis' bedroom to find her hanging upside down in some upside down hanging contraption. "Mavis, who did this to you? Let me get you out of there."

"Granny, relax, it's ok. This thing stretches out my back. I have to be limber for my imagination reality TV show," Mavis explained as she released herself from the contraption.

"I need you to drive me downtown to get my car and don't ask." Granny hurried out to Mavis' garage.

Mavis' car was a brown, 1973 Valiant Sedan that had seen better days. Normally Granny wouldn't be seen in such a car unless her kids were around but this was an exception.

Mavis and Granny drove out of the garage; Granny had to stop herself from impatiently tapping her fingers in anxiety as Mavis drove ten mph to town. Granny knew she could have walked faster than this but she was tired. All this hoopla had worn her out.

Mavis dropped Granny off by her Corvette without asking too many questions.

Granny waved Mavis off and climbed into her car. Her stomach was growling. When had she eaten last? Granny decided to stop at Rack's Restaurant and have a bite to eat before heading home. She drove into Rack's parking lot, avoiding the weeping tree in case darkness fell before she left the restaurant. She pulled into a parking stall right next to a nifty 1957 black Corvette with red trim.

Granny couldn't help it. She had to walk around the black Corvette and admire its workmanship. She had to touch the sleek body. If the door had been unlocked she might have even taken the chance to sit in the driver's seat. Whoever owned that car had class.

Granny took her usual seat in the back of the restaurant next to the window so she could observe everything in and out of the restaurant. Maizie, her usual waitress, came to take her order.

"The usual Granny? Deep fried onion rings, deep fried chicken, mashed potatoes and gravy topped off with chocolate fudge ice cream and a chocolate donut on top?"

"You got it. Add a glass of water and a glass of milk. They tell me milk and water keeps a gal healthy, wealthy and wise." Granny laughed and handed the menu back to Maizie.

Maizie was one in a million. When Granny's kids brought her here, she pretended Granny always ate healthy. She would ask Granny if she wanted her usual baked fish, steamed vegetables, lettuce salad and yogurt for desert. Yes, she was one in a million.

There didn't seem too much going on tonight. There were a few people at the bar and the tables were half full. It seemed to be a quiet night in Fuchsia. Granny noticed the table at the far end of the room. She blushed when she made eye contact with the handsome older man who she seemed to keep falling over. He winked at her first this time. Granny winked back and lowered her head and glanced around wondering if anyone noticed.

As Granny took the time to savor her food bite by bite, she tried to remember the last time her heart had beat a little faster for a member of the opposite sex. The most romantic thing Ferdinand had ever said to her was, "You come from good stock, Hermiony." Granny always wondered if he was talking about the kind of stock as in a stock yard, the stock they have in the grocery store, a corn stalk or the stock they carry in the candy store. Granny always hoped it was the candy store stock.

From time to time, Granny would sneak a glance at the older man. He was probably some old fuddy duddy whose idea of a good time was reading the obituaries in the newspaper. *Nope,* Granny thought, she liked her life as it was.

After devouring her favorite food, Granny paid the check and headed for the door. She forgot about the step up to get to the steps down that led out of the restaurant. She started to tumble head first down the stairs when strong arms caught her. She looked up into the eyes of the handsome older man. Again, he set her on her feet and winked.

"Since you seem to be falling for me all the time perhaps it's time we introduced ourselves. I'm Franklin Gatsby. And you are?"

"Granny, just Granny, nice to meet you. If I have to fall for someone, I'm glad I picked you." Granny realized what she said, blushed, and started out of the restaurant. Franklin followed.

"It's good to meet you, Granny. I'm new around here and don't know too many people. Perhaps you could help me get acquainted with the town."

"Where are you from and why did you pick Fuchsia for your new stomping grounds?" Granny asked, never one to be shy to get details. After all, that was her secret job.

"I moved here from New York. I was a detective with the New York City Police Department. When I retired, I'd always dreamed of moving somewhere quiet where there was beauty and no crime. Fuchsia fit the description."

Granny didn't think it was time to bust his bubble about the crime part so she kept on walking to her car. Franklin kept pace with her.

"This is your car?"

"Yes, do you have a problem with that?" Granny asked, ready to defend herself and her choice of car.

Franklin patted the black 1957 Corvette. "This is my car."

Granny's teeth would have fallen out of her mouth had she had false teeth, but the best she could do was drop open her mouth and stare.

"You have a Corvette? Aren't you a little old for a car like that?"

"That's the cat calling the kettle black," Frank answered back.

Granny hopped into her car still in shock. She gave a wave and squealed off before she could put her foot in her mouth anymore.

As Granny crawled into bed, she decided she needed to go shopping for some new night clothes. Tomorrow morning she'd drive over to Brilliant, Minnesota, and shop at Red Hot Mama's Boutique. She couldn't shop for her nighties in Fuchsia. Small towns were notorious for gossip and word would get around that Granny was trying to relive her youth and her kids would come and cart her away.

Chapter Eleven

Granny had a fun morning shopping at Red Hot Momma's Boutique. They had just gotten in some fuchsia-colored, slinky nighties, edged with pink and purple fur. Granny thought since she was from Fuchsia she should have a fuchsia nightie with fur. They also had black-sequined shortie pajamas that sparkled in the dark. Granny purchased those too, along with the newest bikini they had that had rhinestones around the edges. Of course Granny didn't go swimming, but she could put on the bikini, hop into her bath tub, and pretend she was at a beach in Malibu. No one would know.

As Granny drove back into town, she noticed a lot of hubbub on Main Street. She parked in the We Save You Church's parking lot and walked over to Ella's Enchanted Forest where the hubbub seemed to be taking place. Delight came running to Granny in tears. Granny looked up to see the word "Ella" hanging by a thread to the building. Ella was Delight's daughter and she had named the store after her.

"Granny, look," Delight gestured toward the sign above the door, "Ella is hanging by a thread."

"It's ok, Delight; we can hang it back up."

"No, you don't understand. Someone came into the Enchanted Forest. No locks are broken, no windows smashed. They took my forest, they took Ella. I know they did. She was here closing last night. I haven't heard from her since. They took my forest, all the plants, all the trees and look what they left me, a dilapidated fountain of a cat. Who would do that?"

Granny walked closer to the window, peered in and saw the empty forest and then she spied the fountain of the cat. Granny backed away muttering, "It can't be; it can't be."

"Did you say something, Granny?" Delight asked

"No, no, but I have to check on something. You're in good hands with the Big Guy and the police. I have to go. I have to go."

At that precise moment, the Big Guy walked over and stood beside Granny. "Any thoughts on this, Granny? Where do you supposed that fountain came from? Who would replace a forest with a fountain? I'm gonna catch these crooks if it's the last thing I do."

Granny slowly started backing away. "I'm late, I'm late for a very important skate, um I mean, wait, no date!" Granny quickly turned, dropped the pretense of a limp or walking slowly and sprinted to her car, climbed in and screeched down the street, ignoring the possibility of getting stopped for reckless driving.

Granny almost crashed into her garage in her haste to get to her home. She hopped out of her car, ran into her back yard and stopped short. Her cat statue was gone and in its place were many plants and trees. Granny had a forest in her back yard.

As Granny was trying to get over the shock of the forest, she felt a nip at her ankle. She looked down and along with Fish, the little white poodle and Furball, there was a tank of a dog nipping at her ankle. He had stubby little legs, teeth that didn't fit in his mouth, jowls that seemed to hang down to his chest and beady brown eyes that were staring at her for her attention.

Before Granny could take it all in, she heard the closing of the back yard gate and someone scurrying up behind her.

"Granny, Granny, here you are. Are you alright?"

Granny turned around and looked straight into the face of Gram Gramstead.

"What are you doing here?" Granny used her gruffest voice.

"I saw you tear out of the parking lot of the We Save You Church and I followed you. I thought something might be wrong." Gram proceeded to eye Granny up and down.

Granny wrinkled her nose, put out her arms and said "Stop, don't come any closer. I'm contagious. I'm breaking out with chicken pox."

Gram looked at her suspiciously. "I don't see any chicken pox."

"It's on my stomach." Granny started lifting her shirt. "I didn't realize I was breaking out until I was talking to Delight. Caught it from my Grandkids. Be careful; I'll infect you." She advanced on Gram.

Gram backed up slowly and then turned and literally ran out of the back yard, the fence door slamming loudly behind her.

Granny heaved a sigh of relief and sank down onto the garden bench. She looked at the four creatures sitting in front of her and then lifted her eyes to gaze at the forest that had appeared in her back yard.

How had this happened and why? First, the earrings appeared at her feet and now the forest. Granny knew she was forgetful and foggy but she didn't think she could pull off hiding a forest and transplanting it in her back yard.

Granny lifted her cell phone to dial 911 and then stopped. Would they believe her? She had access to the stores, she had held the earrings, she knew the people who disappeared, and some clues to the disappearance of the jewelry, the appliances, and especially the forest were here in her house. Maybe they'd think she did it. Her kids would be called. Maybe she should turn herself in and plead the fifth.

Actually she thought that possibly she didn't need to plead the fifth. She could say she didn't remember because she didn't. Maybe they'd then take pity on her and send her to the wrinkle factory instead of the hoosegow. Granny got up and paced the patio. What to do? What to do? As she was pacing, Furball jumped on her head, Tank—as she dubbed the strange dog—nipped at her heels, and Fish and the little white poodle seemed to be pacing with her.

Granny stopped pacing, pulled her little 100 lb, 5 foot frame as tall as she could and said to herself, "What is wrong with this picture? Granny giving up? Never!" Granny slammed her cell phone closed and marched out of the back yard, closing the fence gate behind her. She marched straight across the street to Mavis' house. Mavis was sunbathing on her roof. Granny found the ladder and climbed up onto the roof to talk to Mavis. Unlike Granny saving her bikini moments for her bathtub, Mavis didn't have any qualms about sunbathing on her roof in her itsy bitsy, teeny weenie, pink, polka dot bikini.

"Mavis, did you notice anyone coming and going at my house today?"

Mavis lifted her lip-shaped sunglasses and looked at Granny. "Not a soul. I did notice the trees in your backyard grew a lot today. I watched as they slowly peeked above your roof. It's so nice to see some greenery back there now, Granny. You'll have to tell me what kind of seeds you used to produce a forest in such a short time."

"And you didn't think it was strange that trees just automatically started peeking over my house and walk over to investigate?"

"Well, I did wonder about that, but then someone in a car stopped and started taking my picture. I didn't want to move. I was in my perfect picture pose."

Granny shook her head and carefully climbed back down the ladder. As Granny was walking away, she accidently on purpose hooked her umbrella around the ladder's bottom, pulling it to the ground with her.

"Whoops," Granny yelled, "Mavis, your ladder accidently fell and I'm too weak to put it back up. Oh, my, what will we do?" Granny caught Mavis' attention as she sprinted over to George's yard.

"Granny, come back! Granny!" Mavis shouted in exasperation.

"I'll send George over," Granny yelled back.

Granny pounded on George's door. It took George a few minutes to make it to the door. Between his age and his round belly and the fact George never got excited about anything, door answering required a great deal of effort on George's part.

"Hi, Granny, what are you hollering about?"

"I don't know how it happened but Mavis is stuck on her roof. I'm so frail I can't lift the ladder to rescue her. Can you help George?"

"I'll meander over there, Granny." Granny fell in step beside George as he slowly, with the walk of a turtle, made his way to Mavis' house.

"George, did you see anything strange at my house yesterday?"

"Not that I can recall, except for the new mailman. He stopped in front of your house for a long time. He kept staring at your house. I think he was trying to get his lay of the land so he got his addresses right. The postal service doesn't take kindly to its mail men delivering mail to the wrong address."

"What did he look like?"

"Can't describe him exactly. He was a good looking young man. Never saw him before. My daughters would have been swooning over him."

Granny thought he sounded like the young man who had been popping up and watching wherever she went. Was he watching her home too?

Mavis was still yelling like a banshee by the time George and Granny stepped onto her yard.

Granny bid George good-bye, glanced up at Mavis, winked, and proceeded to Sally's place.

When Granny knocked on Sally's door, Sally called to her from the back yard. Sally was pulling weeds in the middle of the yard.

"Sally they have weed killer for that."

"I know, Granny, but I don't want to hurt my grass. Grass is a living thing, you know."

"But you're pulling out the weeds and weeds are a living thing."

"But the grass told me it's having hard time breathing. It says the weeds are choking it."

Granny raised her eyes to the heavens as if to ask for help or something to transport her quickly elsewhere. "Sally, grass does not talk."

"All living things talk if you listen, Granny," Sally softly told her with an angelic expression on her face.

"Sally, did you see anything unusual at my house today."

"Only Baskerville; he must have gotten away from Mrs. Shrill. He was trying to fit his big body into your pet door. He couldn't quite make it. It brought me my laugh for the day. He got stuck. Your little white poodle came behind him and pulled his tail and helped him out. It would have been a perfect *America's Funniest Home Video* moment. Where are Mavis' pretend reality show cameras when you need them?"

Sally handed Granny a bucketful of grass. "Take this home and plant it in your forest that grew today. Your forest will love you for it."

Granny gave up and walked back home with her bucket of grass thinking maybe she was in a bad dream and this would all be gone by tomorrow morning.

Granny was expecting Furball to jump on her when she walked in the door but the house was suspiciously quiet. There were no furry creatures to greet her. She filled eight bowls with food and water expecting the mad dash for food from Fish at least, but it was unusually quiet.

The four troublemakers would eventually come home. Granny hoped this time they'd leave the presents elsewhere. She had all the surprises she could handle for the day. Instead of reaching for her ice cream and donuts, Granny hauled out her bottle of wine and poured herself a full glass of wine. She deserved it. Maybe the wine would help her think clearly about the situation.

Who was this strange young man and why was he watching her? Were the ladies who were missing part of a gang of thieves? Granny hardly could believe Ella would be part of something sinister.

Should they be looking for dead bodies? If the police thought they were part of the heist, they wouldn't be looking for dead bodies or hostages.

How did the thugs get into the store without bothering the alarm or breaking any doors and windows? Granny's mind kept churning with more questions. She poured herself another glass of wine.

Who was this Gram Gramstead woman following her around? She looked so familiar. She was becoming annoying and getting in the way of her investigation. What if she told someone about the forest in Granny's back yard? The last question Granny was in the midst of asking herself was who did all these animals belong to? when the pet door flopped open.

Fish, followed by the little white poodle, followed by Furball, followed by Tank, hurtled into the room. They ran up to Granny and started doing a dance around her chair. Tank dropped a large belt at her feet. "What have you four been up to now?" Granny sighed as eight loveable eyes stared up at her.

All of a sudden, someone started banging on Granny's door. Fish, the little white poodle, Furball and Tank ran and hid under Granny's bed. Granny thought her kids must be here. Fish only moved that fast when Penelope and StarShine were at the door.

Granny picked up her wine glass and her bottle of wine and tossed them in the laundry bag. Her daughters wouldn't wash her clothes at this hour of the night. Granny opened the door.

A fist in midair, ready to pound on the door again, hit Granny's hat knocking it to the ground.

"Franklin?" Granny yelled in her no nonsense voice while trying to catch her hat.

"Granny?" Franklin proclaimed in surprise.

"Franklin, what are you doing here?"

"What are you doing here, Granny?"

"I live here."

"You're the owner of these thieves?" Franklin half shouted trying to keep his very seldom displayed temper in control.

"What thieves?"

Franklin sputtered, "That mangy cat and that half pint of a creature that resembles a miniature mop."

"You had the earrings?" Granny asked suspiciously.

"Earrings, what earrings? I'm talking about Itsy and Bitsy."

Granny looked at Franklin as if he'd lost his mind. "Itsy and Bitsy? I have no idea who Itsy and Bitsy are. I am the only one who lives here along with Fish, little white poodle, Furball and Tank. Now if you'll excuse me, I'm going to retire for the night. Go take your accusatory ranting somewhere else. And to think I winked at you." Granny used her huffiest voice and started to shut the door.

Franklin gently stopped her and in his gentlest detective voice, pleaded with Granny to let him in. "Apparently we have some sort of misunderstanding. Perhaps we could talk about this." And then he winked at Granny.

Granny blushed, hesitated and opened the door. "I suppose I should give you a chance to explain yourself."

Franklin walked in and picked up Furball. "This is Itsy." He then picked up Tank. "This is Bitsy."

Granny gave him an incredulous look and started laughing. "That huge fur ball you call Itsy. And I have news for you; Tank is a boy. Bitsy? You're kidding me, right?" With that, Granny couldn't hold it in any longer. She practically rolled on the floor in laughter.

Franklin started to sputter and then he too started laughing. When they finally could control themselves, Franklin explained, "These were my daughter's dog and cat. She named them. I inherited them when she grew up and moved away. Your Fish and your little white poodle lured them out of my home. I'd been wondering where they had been going at night. They show up during the day and then disappear. Today, I watched and saw these two little shysters steal my belt, and lure Itsy and

Bitsy away, so I followed them. It led me to your doorstep."

"And you don't know anything about any earrings?"

"I don't wear earrings. Why would I have earrings at my house?" Franklin asked in bewilderment.

"Never mind, just a question from a foggy old lady."

"Young lady, you're only as old as you let yourself be."

Granny thought to herself, *If he only knew*.

"I will take Itsy and Bitsy and head for home. I'll take my belt too, if you don't mind." he said, picking the belt up off of the floor. Franklin paused as he stepped outside the door and turned to Granny. "Um, would you care to have dinner with me some evening?"

Granny, startled by the invitation, thought about it a second, "I'll check my schedule and get back to you. Perhaps, I'll fall for you downtown tomorrow morning at Ella's Enchanted Forest while I'm having my latte. If you happen to be there I'll give you my answer then." Granny winked a shy wink and closed the door on him.

Franklin Jester Gatsby, named Jester by his aunts because as a baby he was unknowingly, like babies are, always entertaining them with his foolish antics, almost lost his grip on Itsy and Bitsy as Granny shut the door in his face.

He turned away and walked to his car. Whispering softly to Itsy and Bitsy, he said, "Haven't met a woman like that since my mama graced this earth. And one mama on this earth was enough for a lifetime of women." Franklin also wondered why he'd asked Granny to dinner. She was trouble with a capitol T and he knew he should let trouble be. Franklin hesitated as he got into his car, now he was rhyming just like Granny. Quickly he headed for the nearest watering hole aka bar. He needed a stiff drink and time to think.

Granny leaned against the closed door and with closed eyes and a smile on her face, she briefly pictured herself planting a big kiss on Franklin. She chuckled as she visualized his surprise.

With a little sigh, Granny turned away from the door and leaned down, patted Fish and little white poodle as they sadly whined at the loss of their friends. Granny looked at the little white poodle. "I guess I should try and find out who you belong too. Perhaps then I won't have any more surprises at my door in the middle of the night."

Granny checked on her neighbors, put her package from Red Hot Mama's Boutique by her bed, threw herself on her bed and promptly fell asleep in her clothes. She was too pooped to even think about trying out her new nighttime attire.

Chapter Twelve

Granny slept soundly. Granny was in the middle of dreaming about painting her house pink and adding a secret room upstairs in her home where she could run her Pinkster Detective Agency, when a door closing woke her up.

Granny looked down to see if it would be safe to venture out of her room and then she remembered she'd slept in her clothes last night. Her kids would think she was already up and dressed for the day.

Granny found a note and some weird sweeper, washer object, sitting in her kitchen.

"Hi, Mom," It was a note from Starshine.

"I didn't want to wake you up. I was driving through Fuchsia and wanted to drop off this floor scrubber to make your life easier. I know the last time we were here you were using bowls because buckets were too hard for you to manage to scrub your floor (this time I see you had eight bowls out). Enjoy."

Granny examined the floor scrubber and felt a little sheepish pulling the wool over her children's eyes. The feeling didn't last very long. You gotta do what ya gotta do was Granny's motto.

Starshine had such a soft heart. She took after her name. Granny didn't have the heart to tell her that the way she dressed reminded Granny of the hippy era. Granny must have been clairvoyant when she named Starshine after the song in the musical *Hair*. Starshine always twinkled with her sparkly eyes, eyes that seemed to twinkle all the way deep into her soul. One look at Starshine and everyone fell in love with that twinkle and her soft heart. One time Starshine stopped and waited in the middle of the road for a bird to finish picking up the grain a farmer had dropped from his wagon. Granny urged her to just go and Starshine replied, "He has the right to eat too, Mom. What is my time worth compared to that of a hungry little creature?" Granny learned early on to accept Starshine's soft ways, even if that did mean pretending to love a floor scrubber.

Granny had decided on a plan of action before she had crashed into a deep sleep on her bed last night. She was going to examine every store for unknown nooks and crannies that the thieves could have been hiding in. Maybe they left a clue. Maybe she could discover who the good looking young man was. She was going to have to be overly vigilant.

Granny put her usual umbrella in her closet and pulled out her expensive, long handled, double crooked umbrella with the triple spikes on the ends. She needed to be well armed if she ran into trouble in those nooks and crannies. Then she emptied her pocketbook into the larger, steel handled, tin rimmed, designer pocketbook with the extra weights in the bottom for a backup hit em' over the header.

Granny pulled down her long socks, plopped on her hat, pulled out the strands of hair, disheveled her clothes and walked out to her garage hoping her car was there.

Granny opened the door to her garage an inch at a time and then stuck her head through the crack in the door, in case she was disappointed and her car had disappeared again. It would be easier to fall in shock on the soft grass rather than the concrete floor. Her eyes zeroed in on her car, sitting shining in the sun, as the sun glinted through the garage window. With a whoop, Granny opened the door all the way, hit the button on the garage door opener, hopped in her car, revved the engine and squealed out of her garage almost knocking over her mailbox at the end of her driveway as she made too tight a turn trying to avoid over shooting the street and backing straight into Mavis' house.

As Granny drove to town, she passed Mrs. Shrill's house. Baskerville was not out. *Too bad*, she thought she might lure Baskerville to her car and give him some of the treats she'd stashed under her car seat. It would wake her up a little more to hear a good, loud, "tut, tut, tut," from Mrs. Shrill.

Granny parked in front of AbStract. She grabbed her umbrella and her pocketbook. She no more than walked in the door of AbStract when she felt a tap on her shoulder. It was Gram Gramstead.

"I've been patiently waiting for you. I thought we should shop together today."

Granny had to think quickly. "That sounds lovely but I don't have a lot of time today. Maybe you could help me find what I'm looking for and save me time."

"Of course, Granny; what can I do?"

"I was going to drive over to Allure to see if the Big Box electronic store over there had any 60" televisions since the ones in Fuchsia got stolen. My eyes are so bad I just can't watch my itty bitty screen anymore. If you could go over there and price them for me, I could get my errands done. We could meet at Rack's tonight for dinner, my treat."

Granny really didn't want to do the dinner thing with Gram because she knew she'd be worn out from all her sleuthing and she was very suspicious of Gram, but she couldn't sleuth if Gram was following her. And she couldn't have a latte with Franklin if Gram was following her. She didn't want Gram to start winking at Franklin.

"I could do that. I've wanted to head to Allure to see if I could find a purse to match my hair. They don't seem to have any this color in Fuchsia. I'll meet you at Rack's at 5:00 p.m." With that, Gram sped out the door.

Granny gave a sigh of relief. She headed to the jewelry counter. Justine was polishing the jewelry.

"Hi, Justine, any word about Estelle?"

"No, Granny, the police think she was in on the heist. But, Granny, I'm worried. I don't think Estelle would do anything like that but I can't get them to believe me. Estelle wouldn't just disappear like that."

"I agree, Justine. Did they recover some of the jewelry? The case is full again."

"No, insurance picked up the tab. Business has been brisk since the heist. Everyone comes in because they are curious about the robbery and Justine's disappearance. They always buy something. Who could resist these gorgeous gems?"

"Me," Granny laughed, "they're out of my price range." Granny took her time and limped down the aisles. Granny walked to the corner where she'd seen the good looking young man. Checking to see that no one was watching her, she started tapping on the walls and floor with her umbrella. As she was making her way around the little corner she saw a movement out of the corner of her eye. When she glanced up she saw the good looking young man watching her from across the room. Granny was quick; she raised her umbrella, started spinning herself around, gave the umbrella a good swing, pushed her remote button and tossed the umbrella across the room of the store.

When her body quit spinning from whirling the umbrella around, there was no young man in her line of vision, there was only a swath of toppled shelves and purses. Her umbrella had come to land on the jewelry case after hitting a chandelier and three arrangements of purses that stood on the shelves in the middle of the room. Justine, who was standing by the jewelry counter, was staring at her with an open mouth.

The Big Guy came running, looking around to arrest the thief that Granny had caught. When he didn't see anyone to cuff, he turned to Granny with a, what's up with this? look.

Granny hung her head and loudly proclaimed, "I got dizzy, the room started spinning. As it started spinning, I started spinning and my umbrella got away from me. My weak arms couldn't hold it and it flew across the room." Granny winked at Big Guy.

Big Guy whispered to Granny. "Granny, there's no one to arrest. Would you mind explaining this mess?"

"Well, there was someone. He was young and good looking and he was watching me."

"Did you see him trying to steal anything?"

"Well no," Granny answered slowly, "But I knew he was going to." Slowly Granny started backing out of the store.

"I have an appointment at Ella's Enchanted Forest and I can't be late." Granny hustled faster so the Big Guy couldn't protest.

Was she imagining this good looking young man always watching her? She couldn't be. He sounded exactly like the mailman sitting in front of her house. Granny decided she'd check with the post office later in the day to see if she had a new mailman.

Cornelius aka the Big Guy, watched Granny limp out the door using her umbrella as a cane. "Justine, did you see the young man that Granny was referring to?"

"No, all I saw was the umbrella with its spikes heading towards my head. I was afraid I was going to end up with more holes in my body besides just my ears when I saw that umbrella spinning. Granny spins a mean umbrella."

Cornelius turned back to the door thoughtfully. Perhaps he should keep a better eye on Granny. Maybe it was time for her to retire.

When Granny walked in to the Enchanted Forest, Franklin was waiting for her with fresh donuts on the table, a latte for him in one hand, and one for her in the other. He winked at Granny as she sat down.

"Busy morning, Granny?"

"You might say that. How are Furball and Tank?" I missed them last night after you left."

"Itsy and Bitsy are fine and so are your Fish and your little white poodle."

Granny screwed up her eyes and squinted at him. "And you know this how?"

"I fed them Beef and Chicken tidbits for breakfast this morning at my house."

"They were at your house? They aren't supposed to have Beef and Chicken. They are supposed to have Tofu and Yogurt and vegetables. You want to kill them with that unhealthy meat?"

Franklin ignored Granny's censure about the food and got straight to the point. "The point being, what are we going to do about this situation between Itsy, Bitsy, Fish and little white poodle?"

Granny stood up. "I don't see that we have a situation and it's Furball and Tank. It's time you gave those creatures respectable names. It will give them courage. Friday night! Dinner! You let me know when and where and I'll be there," Granny chuckled at the rhyme and walked out the door to continue her investigation. She only had so much time before that pesky Gram would show up.

Franklin watched Granny walk out the door and down the street. He wondered if he should follow her. She intrigued him with her strange ways.

Franklin Jester Gatsby wasn't sure he was up to any more drama. That was why he had left New York City and come to Fuchsia. He wanted a quiet life with no drama. He missed his wife. She'd been a quiet influence in his life. His wife had been so different than his mother. Granny was so much like his mother that it scared him.

His wife's restful soul had kept him sane during his crazy life as a New York City Detective. Once she died, the craziness got to be too much for him. Even though he hadn't spent much time at home and his wife had almost single handedly raised his daughters by herself, she was the calm in the midst of the storm where he could safely rest.

Franklin's eyes still followed Granny. Deep in thought, he swallowed his last swig of coffee and walked out the door in the opposite direction of Granny. He wondered why if she scared him so much, because she was like his mother, that he felt so excited and alive when he was sparring with her.

Chapter Thirteen

When Granny walked into Rack's Restaurant, Gram Gramstead was already seated at Granny's favorite spot at the back of the room. Granny squared her shoulders, gritted her teeth, sighed, and made her way to the back of the restaurant to where Gram was seated.

"You made it, Granny. I had such an exciting day. They have all kinds of 60" televisions in Allure. I made a list and also took pictures. I stopped at home and printed it out on my computer so you could have a copy too." Gram pushed the list at Granny.

Before Granny could speak, Gram continued on, "Let me know which television you choose. I decided I'd buy one just like yours. Oh, and I already ordered the food for us."

Granny's hand started to squeeze tighter on her umbrella. She took a deep breath to get her ire under control. Finally, when she felt she could speak in a reasonable voice, she asked "And where are you from, Gram? You look very familiar. Have we met before this last week?"

As Granny waited for an answer, Maizie arrived with their meal. Gram had ordered for herself, deep fried onion rings, deep fried chicken, mashed potatoes and gravy. On the side was chocolate fudge ice cream with a chocolate donut on top. As Granny stared at Gram's choice of food, Maizie put the food Gram had ordered for Granny in front of Granny.

Maizie looked at Granny with a concerned look. "Granny when Gram ordered your meal she explained you were trying to stabilize your health and you had to change your diet. I'm sorry to hear that you're having problems."

Granny stared at Maizie as Maizie set her food down in front of her. Granny glanced down at the plate that was supposed to be her dinner. On the plate was some kind of steamed fish, steamed broccoli, steamed carrots and yogurt for desert.

Granny held on tighter to her umbrella with a death grip. Her hand was shaking, wanting to lift that umbrella and tangle it in Gram's red hair. With a gulp, Granny turned to Maizie. "You're glowing tonight Maizie," and then Granny noticed Maize's earrings. They were almost an exact replica of the Junkyard earrings stolen from AbStract, and an almost replica of the earring that was now hidden in Granny's house. "And those are to die for earrings,"

Granny remarked. Granny watched Maizie's face carefully as she answered.

Maizie blushed and started giggling. "I've met someone. He's so handsome and he gave me these earrings as an "I want to get to know you better" present. He's right over there. Would you like to meet him?" Maizie gestured to the bar area but when they looked over, there was no one there. "He was just here. I wonder what happened to him. He was going to wait until I closed up tonight and see me safely home. He must have forgotten something in his car." Maizie filled up their water and milk glasses and continued on to her other tables.

Again Granny started to ask Gram if they'd met when Gram exclaimed, "That man at that table just put the salt and pepper shakers, the napkins, the silverware and the ketchup bottle in his wife's purse. Do you believe that?"

Granny grabbed her umbrella, pushed the remote for the Big Guy, and limped to the table. "Oh my, I feel faint," Granny murmured to the man and woman sitting at the table. As she pretended to faint, her umbrella hit the wine glasses sitting on the table. The red wine spilled onto the man's suit and onto the woman's white dress. "Oh no, I'm so sorry," Granny proclaimed and then her umbrella hooked the salt and pepper shakers and the ketchup bottle sitting on the table, shaking the salt and pepper on the man and spilling the ketchup on the woman's white dress.

The Big Guy ran in ready with his handcuffs and cuffed the man and the woman. "What did they do?" he asked Granny.

"That woman, Gram Gramstead, saw them putting the napkins, the salt and pepper shakers and the ketchup in the woman's purse."

The Big Guy cleared his throat. "Granny, you just spilled the salt and pepper shakers, the wine and the ketchup on these poor people. If they stole them by putting them in this poor woman's purse, they wouldn't be laying here in their laps from your umbrella assault."

Granny pointed to her table at the back of the restaurant. "But she said...." As Granny pointed, she looked to her table and it was empty. Gram was nowhere to be seen.

The Big Guy apologized to the people and explained the restaurant would pay for any damage and escorted Granny outside. "Do you need help getting home, Granny? Perhaps you've been pushing yourself too hard. You aren't getting any younger. Go home; get a good night's sleep. I'll visit you in the morning and we'll talk about these little mistakes we've had lately."

Granny shook free of his arm. "I'm fine. I'm not making this up. I'll prove it to you." Granny started stalking off to her car when she remembered the Big Guy said he was coming by in the morning. Granny couldn't let that happen. He'd see the forest; he might notice the earrings. She turned, looked the Big Guy in the eye and said, "I'll come to you and we'll talk. 9:00 a.m., Rack's. Be there or be square." Granny jumped in her car and slowly drove away.

When Granny walked in her door, she had a surprise waiting for her. Fish, little white poodle, Furball and Tank were all there to greet her. She patted them all and said to Furball and Tank, "You guys running away from home again?" Granny let out a roar of laughter finding it funny that they'd outsmarted Franklin.

"And you didn't even bring me any unexpected presents. That's good. I don't I think I could've handled another surprise today. Maybe Big Guy is right. Maybe my kids are right. I have to think this out."

Granny plopped in her chair, kicked her sparkly shoes off, revealing her purple polka dot socks that she had on over her old woman stockings. The tops of her sparkly shoes kept the socks hidden. It gave her an impish thrill to think she was fooling everyone with her respectable clothes. She was so tired her eyes closed and she started dreaming that it was raining chocolates when there was a light knock on the door.

It took Granny a minute to remember where she was. She reluctantly pulled herself out of the chair to answer the door. Wearily, she opened the door.

"Franklin, what are you doing here?"

In answer, Franklin held up a fuchsia, fur-trimmed nightie!

Granny's eyes opened wide. She gave Franklin her owl stare. Granny felt the red creeping up her body into her face as she blushed in nervousness. And then she slammed the door right in Franklin's face.

"Granny, let me in or I'll pound on this door all night. I'll hang this on the mailbox in front of your house if you don't let me in."

Granny took a deep breath, straightened her clothes, settled her hat squarely on her head and opened the door.

She looked Franklin squarely in the eyes, "I don't know why you're bringing that fur floozy thing to me." Granny started to shut the door.

Franklin quickly squeezed in before the door shut, which wasn't an easy feat for such a big man. He looked down to see eight little eyes staring at him from under the couch.

"Those shysters, and I include my Itsy and Bitsy in that description, left me this present today."

Granny turned and gave her four furry companions hiding under the couch the evil eye.

Franklin held up the fuchsia, fur-trimmed nightie. "They seem to think I needed this. Since it definitely won't fit me and isn't my color, we know they didn't bring it for me to wear. They wanted me to follow them. I followed them here. Since this is usually the scene of the crime, (Granny turned white when he used the word *crime*), I decided it must be yours."

Granny thought Franklin was enjoying this exchange too much. The grin on his face was growing wider by the minute. What should she do?

Granny grabbed the fuchsia nightie out of Franklin's hand and stuffed it under the sofa cushion. "Maybe it's mine. What of it? You can go now and I won't be hearing any of this on the street or I'll go after you with my umbrella."

Granny stomped over to the door and held it wide open.

Franklin sat down on the couch. "You better close the door, Granny, or someone might hear our conversation and know your secret."

Granny blanched and turned white. "What secret?" she asked anxiously.

"That you wear wild nighties. Granny, at your age what would everyone think?" Franklin let out a big, loud, chuckle and winked at Granny.

Granny slammed the door.

"I think we need to get a few things straight, Granny. The first thing, apparently our furry friends like each other, so let them spend the day here and the nights at my house like they've been doing. We can share them. That way we can keep an eye on their mischievous ways. Secondly, I kind of like you. I think you're kind of cute. So I won't tell anyone your secret but you have to have dinner with me."

Franklin got up and opened the door. He turned to Granny. "And I like fuchsia nighties." Laughing, he winked, walked through the door into the night. Abruptly he stopped, turned, gave Granny another wink, smiled broadly at Granny and closed the door.

Granny slowly sat down on the couch. Fish, the little white poodle, Furball, and Tank guiltily crawled out from underneath the couch toward the pet door.

"Stop! Wherever you're going, I don't want any more presents. You won't take any presents to Franklin either. Do you understand?" All four looked at her, and scurried as fast as they could out the pet door.

Granny grabbed the fuchsia nightie from under the cushion, grabbed a box of chocolates and headed to bed. This day was enough to give an old woman heart flutters

.

Chapter Fourteen

Granny had just been about to receive the key to the city for stopping a gang of mobsters from robbing the bank when the ring of the phone stopped the dream right as the Mayor was presenting her with the key to the city of Fuchsia.

"What! You interrupted the presentation ceremony," Granny yelled into the phone.

Mrs. Shrill shouted, "Do you know what's going on downtown, Granny?"

"Tut, tut, tut," Granny shouted into the phone before she slammed down the receiver. She didn't know why Mrs. Shrill continued to call her to give her news of the day. The only conversation they ever had was "Tut, tut, tut."

Granny checked the color of her big toe before climbing out of bed. She was so tired from the goings on of yesterday that she didn't even check to see if there was children noise in the house. She staggered to the kitchen to pour herself a glass of wine for breakfast. It wasn't something she usually did. She usually saved the wine for an evening treat but what the heck! At her age she needed to do something out of the ordinary to get her started for the day. She had the feeling it was going to be longer than yesterday.

When Granny checked on George with her binoculars she noticed that every morning he hung out a different wildly colored pair of boxer shorts. This was something new the past few weeks.

Mavis was surprisingly mellow in her reality show this morning. When she saw that Granny was checking on her she raised a cup of coffee to the window and took a sip.

Sally's shade was up. She was probably out in her lawn talking to her grass.

Granny fed Fish, the little white poodle, Furball and Tank before she left the house. Walking to the garage to get her car she noticed the forest seemed to be growing and it would tower over her house soon and be very noticeable. She had to figure this out soon or she'd be trading in her fuchsia nightie for an orange jumpsuit.

When Granny opened the door to the garage, all the doors on her car were open and so was the trunk. Granny stopped, lifted her umbrella and her pocketbook, ready to strike any unwanted person that might be lurking.

She did the swat team dance around the garage checking the corners and looking under the car. All clear. Granny started to close the doors on her car but when she got to her trunk she looked in. There in her trunk were five bottles of wine. Granny checked out the label. This was expensive wine.

Granny shook her head as if to clear her mind. Did she buy the wine and forget? She wouldn't buy this wine. It was too expensive. Why was this wine in her trunk? Had Franklin planted it? After all, what did she really know about Franklin? Had his visit been an excuse to plant the wine as evidence, but as evidence of what? Granny lifted the bottle and contemplated popping the cork. Somehow that idea seemed safer than heading downtown to see what was going on. Granny put the bottle back in her trunk regrettably, deciding she better not shirk her duties. She didn't want to get fired from her detective work.

Granny slammed the trunk shut. She'd have to deal with it later. She had to get to town to see what Mrs. Shrill had been flapping about. Her meeting with the Big Guy would have to wait.

Granny hopped into the driver's seat. Her keys were still there. *It couldn't have been too smart an intruder*, Granny thought as she started the car and drove out of the garage. Who would leave bottles of wine and not take a vintage 1957 Corvette?

As Granny pulled into a parking stall on Main Street, she noticed that the police, the fire trucks and the ambulance were in the parking lot of Rack's Restaurant. That must have been what Mrs. Shrill was yapping about.

Granny walked over to the Big Guy who was standing in front of Racks. Granny pretended to trip over her umbrella so the Big Guy could catch her and they had an excuse to talk.

"Again, another break in?" Granny whispered.

"Same scenario, Granny. No locks are broken, no alarms set off. This time they got away with the entire stock of wine. Some of it was some pretty pricy and rare stuff that Racks stored in the wine cellar. This time a fire started in the dumpster. Someone tossed this burning fuschia nightie in the dumpster and started the trash on fire. That's what alerted us to the break in.

We just don't know how the thieves are doing it. And Maizie is missing and so are all the cash register receipts from the night—$10,000 worth. We found Maizie's earring behind the bar. She was supposed to close up last night. We can't find her anywhere. I know I'm missing something. The earrings have to be the connection," he told Granny as he helped her to her feet.

Granny turned ghost white and stumbled a little as the Big Guy helped her to her feet. The words *fuschia nightie, earrings* and *connection* rolled around in her brain as she had a brief flash of the Big Guy hooking the handcuffs around her wrists as he helped her up.

"Granny, Granny, you're as white as a ghost. Perhaps I better call your kids."

"Just give me a minute," Granny said in a weak tone.

Granny looked at the bit of scrap the Big Guy was holding in his hand. "How do you know that's a fuschia nightie?"

"The tag was all that was left when we put the fire out. We traced it to a store called Red Hot Mama's and they confirmed what it was. They're checking their records as we speak."

Granny turned away from the big guy, quickly pinched her cheeks which immediately brought the color back to her cheeks as it was a hard pinch, and turned back to confront the Big Guy again.

Granny glanced at the restaurant window. The good looking young man was watching her from the window.

She grabbed the Big Guy and pointed toward the window. "Do you see that man?" When she looked back, the good looking young man was gone.

"There's no one there, Granny. This time we have the entrances sealed. No one can get in."

"But I saw him. He was there. He's always watching me!" Granny proclaimed in her loudest voice. The ambulance crew, the fire crew and the police turned to look at Granny.

The Big Guy took Granny's arm and led her to a nearby bench. "Granny, are you ok? Let me help you to your car. I think you're not well. I was worried about you after the last restaurant incident."

"I saw this young man. He was in the window. It's not my imagination! I don't need help to my car." To make her point, Granny brought the end of her umbrella right down on his foot.

As Granny did that, she remembered that the Big Guy had said the wine stock had been stolen and she remembered the wine in the trunk of her car.

"I think I need to go home and rest," Granny said just as the Big Guy was trying hard not to let out a yell of pain.

Granny sprinted to her car and drove away as quickly as she could, trying not to draw any suspicion to her car.

The Big Guy watched Granny drive away. He wondered if he should call her kids. Granny's instincts had always been good. That was why the merchants hired her. Who would suspect Granny of being an undercover person for the police department? But lately she was acting stranger than usual.

Granny drove into her garage. She took the bottles of wine, grabbed a shovel, went into her new forest and dug a hole deep enough to bury the wine. She then took the grass that Sally had given her and dumped it on top of the shoveled-in hole. It was at that moment Granny heard a sound. She turned around and bumped straight into Gram Gramstead.

"Hi, Granny."

Granny quickly sat down on top of the lump of grass she'd just patted down to cover the hole she'd dug.

"What are you doing here, Gram?"

"I saw you rush away from the scene of the crime at Rack's so I wanted to make sure you were ok?"

Granny stared intently at Gram's face. There was something about that face. "You always seem to be lurking, Gram. I had to get home to put in my grass before it got dark."

Gram handed Granny a bouquet of flowers. "I brought you some flowers in hopes it would make you feel better. See you later, Granny." Gram turned around and walked out the gate.

Granny stood up and took a whiff of the flowers. That's the last thing Granny remembered doing before she woke up on the ground to Fish, the little white poodle, Furball and Tank licking her face. She must have been sleeping a little while because it was now dark.

Granny sat up confused. Had she fallen asleep in her yard? She still felt groggy. She felt like she'd woken up from a long winter's nap. She remembered smelling the flowers and that was it, except she didn't see any flowers now.

Maybe all this excitement was wearing her out. Maybe there was something to that saying "Wake up and smell the roses." She was smelling roses now and other flower blends too in her imagination.

Then Granny remembered the reason she was in her forest. She'd hid evidence from the crime at Rack's. The wine had to have come from Rack's. Granny made it into the house and plunked down on the couch.

She looked down at Furball. Furball plunked something down in her lap. It was the earring Maizie was wearing when she waited on Granny's table. Granny was looking at the earring in amazement when she heard a rap at the door.

Granny stomped to the door. "What now?" she yelled in irritation, thinking Franklin was on the other side. Granny stepped back with a look of exasperation only to find the Big Guy on the other side of the door.

"Big Guy, what are you doing here?" Granny asked as she gave a glance around her house making sure there was no evidence in clear view. She stuffed the earring she was holding in her pocket so he wouldn't see.

"Granny, we need to talk about these heists. I have some concerns."

"Of course, anything I can help you with. Do you need me to do some undercover sleuthing at night?"

"No, Granny, it's been brought to my attention that at each of these of heists your red Corvette was seen sitting outside the building at closing time. In fact it's sitting in front of Persnickety's Book Store right now."

"It isn't. It's sitting in my garage. I drove it home from Rack's this afternoon. Don't you remember? You were there."

"Yes, I know you weren't feeling well and you were confused. You were seeing people that weren't there."

"He was there!" Granny shouted, "and my car is in my garage! I'll show you." Granny grabbed his arm and proceeded to drag him to her garage as much as you could drag a big hulk like the Big Guy. When Granny opened the door, she stopped short. Her car was not there!

"Look, Granny, this doesn't look good. Do you want me to drive your car home?"

"No, you can give me a ride and I'll drive it home myself." Putting on her most put-out expression, Granny proceeded to his car and plopped herself in the front seat not saying a word until they stopped in front of Granny's car.

"I will prove to you I had nothing to do with this." Granny slammed the door and proceeded to her car.

"I hope you will, Granny. I hope you will."

Granny drove home, parked her car in the garage, double locked her garage door and was thankful it was dark so Big Guy didn't see the forest in her backyard. He would have hauled her away. Her kids would haul her away to the wrinkle farm.

Granny was greeted by the four shysters. They hadn't left for the evening while Granny was out. Granny took turns throwing them treats and thinking about her situation. Furball took that time to jump on her head and purr and that was when Granny had her next light bulb moment. Granny decided to sleep in her clothes. She had her umbrella and pocketbook ready by the bed so she could get going bright and early in the morning. She heard the pet door swish as she formulated her plan in her mind.

Chapter Fifteen

Bright and early the next morning, Granny was pounding on Franklin Gatsby's front door. She'd looked up his address on the internet since he hadn't provided Granny with that information on his recent visit.

Granny's pounding got louder and louder. Where was that man? It was taking him a long time to answer his door and Granny wanted to make sure she wasn't too late.

The door finally opened and when Granny got a look at Franklin, her hand ready to pound again, stopped in midair. Granny's mouth fell open and then she doubled over in a rolling, loud laugh.

"What are you doing here, Granny and what do you think is so funny?" Franklin said with a scowl on his face.

"Why Franklin, a big man like you wearing a fuchsia robe covered with pictures of Furball and Tank? I don't know. What could be funny about that?" With a loud snort, Granny again started into a rolling laugh, laughing louder and louder until she was almost crying.

The door started to shut in her face. "Wait, wait, I need to make sure I'm not too late." Granny stopped for a moment and thought she was getting pretty good at this rhyming stuff. She continued on. "Are the shysters still here?"

"They are. You came all the way over here to ask that question when they'll be back at your house later today. They just had their breakfast. Fish and Itsy had gourmet salmon and Bitsy and little white poodle had steak."

"You fed them steak and salmon? Breakfast is tofu!"

Franklin rolled his eyes. "You are here why?"

Granny looked at Franklin and used every ounce of restraint in her tiny little body to keep herself from laughing at the sight of this big man wearing a fuchsia robe with Furball and Tank all over it.

"First, where did you get that robe? I would have never guessed you were the fuchsia type."

"My daughters gave it to me. I was a little horrified when I opened their present, but after wearing it, I like it. It gets me in touch with my softer side. Do you want to make something of it?" Franklin asked in a huffy voice. "And quit trying to change the subject. Why are you here?"

"I'm here to follow the shysters when they leave your house." As Granny said that, Fish, the little white poodle, Furball and Tank were heading for the pet door. Granny prepared to follow.

Franklin saw what was happening and stepped in front of the pet door and locked it.

"No one leaves this house until you tell me what's going on!"

Fish, the little white poodle, Furball and Tank all turned their backs on Franklin and sat down in a pout.

"You're the big hotshot, retired detective from New York," Granny declared. "You figure it out!"

Granny started over to unlatch the pet door. Franklin stood firmly in front of the pet door. The shysters turned around and looked at Franklin. Fish and Furball hissed loudly, Tank nipped at his ankle and little white poodle sat up in her cutest pose begging him to open the door.

Franklin stood firm, giving Granny the no nonsense, you're not leaving here until you tell me look.

"I need to follow them and see where they go from here."

"Why?"

"Because they keep bringing me presents and I want to see where they shop. Now let them go." Granny started to get agitated and she stomped her umbrella down on the floor.

Again, Granny got up to unhook the pet door. Franklin again, was just as quick to re-latch the hook.

Granny was getting more agitated by the minute. She started pacing and the explanation that she never intended to come out of her mouth just spewed out in a babbling story.

"I have a secret life. I'm an undercover detective for the stores here in town. I catch their crooks."

"What day is this today, Granny? How old are you? Where do you live?" Franklin asked to test her fogginess.

"I know what day it is. I know how old I am. I know where I live. I may be foggy some time, but I'm not senile and I'm not making my job up!" Granny shouted.

She went on and this time Franklin couldn't calm Granny down or interrupt the story she started to tell.

"It started with AbStract being robbed and Estelle disappearing and Estelle's earring ending up at my house as a present from Fish. And then he brought home the little white poodle and then I saw this good looking man watching me in AbStract, only he wasn't, cause he disappeared and no one else saw him," Granny rambled on, one sentence turning into another not always making sense.

"My car was there and then it wasn't and then Ella's Enchanted Forest was robbed and

Delight's daughter Ella was missing and then the forest that got stolen ended up in my backyard and the young man was watching me again and then he wasn't. When Rack's got broken into there were wine bottles in my car. Maizie went missing and her earring ended up in my house and the bottles of wine were from the stock that was stolen from Rack's and so I buried them in my back yard and then I fainted or something and when I came to the shysters were licking my face and I thought I had flowers in my hand and then I didn't. Did I dream them? And then the Big Guy came and he told me my car had been seen in front of the stores the nights of all the robberies, only it wasn't because it was in my garage but it wasn't when I looked, it was at Persnickety's and they are going to haul me away and trade in my fuchsia nightie for an orange jumpsuit, only I'm innocent and the shysters keep bringing me presents that get me in trouble and I have to figure it out. Orange isn't my color." Granny finally took a huge breath and headed to unlock the pet door.

Franklin took a firm grip on Granny's arms and gently lowered her to a chair and got her a glass of milk.

"Granny, let me help you sort this out. Take a breath."

"No one will believe me. I'm little foggy at times. Maybe I did do it? Why can't I remember where the flowers came from and where they went? If I can't remember that, maybe I don't remember stealing all those things? Do I need to go to the wrinkle farm?" Granny looked up at Franklin helplessly.

Franklin thought for a moment. "If you're determined to follow the shysters because you're convinced they know somethin, then let's think this thing out first. What time do they leave your house at night?"

"They swish out the pet door between 10:00 and 11:00 p.m."

"They arrive here at around 2:00 or 3:00 a.m. and they leave again around 7:30 a.m."

"They arrive back at my house sometime in the late afternoon. Usually after 4:00. At least that's the time I've noticed them arriving when I'm home." Granny gave Franklin a stubborn look. "When I'm working my undercover job (Franklin gave Granny a disbelieving look), they're usually waiting for me when I arrive home between 5:00 and 6:00."

"That leaves them a lot of time to get into mischief." Franklin surmised. "After listening to your rambling story I have to ask; how do you think you or anyone else could steal a forest and put it in your back yard?"

"It happened!" Granny screamed in exasperation.

Franklin thought for a moment, wanting to appease Granny. "Ok, Granny, you follow the shysters. After all, what kind of trouble could you get into following them? I'll spin by your back yard and check out your forest and the wine you buried in your back yard. We'll meet back at your place when you follow the shysters to your house.

"But we have to be clever. Those shysters are smart," he whispered. "If they know you're following them, they won't take their regular route. Pretend to leave and go outside and hide in the bush around the corner. I'll give you a few minutes, and then I'll unlatch the pet door. They won't suspect a thing."

Granny stomped her umbrella on the ground, swung her pocketbook wide and in a loud voice announced, "If you don't believe me Franklin Gatsby, I'm leaving!" With a huffy gait, she walked out the door, slamming it on the way out, and hid in the bushes.

A few minutes later, the foursome navigated out the pet door and turned on Blue Bird Lane that led to the lake. Granny followed a distance behind.

Franklin got into his 1957 black Corvette and headed to Granny's back yard.

Bluebird Lake was in the middle of Blue Bird Park. As Granny headed toward the park, making sure the shysters didn't see her, she smiled at the geese that inhabited the lake and the park. Besides being known as the colorful town with the colorful name, Fuchsia was also known for the prolific numbers of geese that inhabited the town. If there was a goose joke anywhere, it always seemed to end up having something to do with Fuchsia. The founding fathers didn't like being known as the goose joke of Minnesota, so they dubbed the Park and the Lake, Blue Bird although Granny couldn't remember the last time she'd seen a blue bird in the park, only geese. Fuchsia was also home to the BlueBird Songbirds Basketball Team and The Blue Bird Raisin Eaters Football Team. Granny's personal opinion was that city folks probably didn't know the difference between geese and blue birds. She always told city folk visitors the geese were blue birds that wear camouflage and they always nodded in agreement.

Granny followed Fish, the little white poodle, Furball and Tank around the lake, back through the park. They started heading to Main Street. They walked with a purpose, in a straight line with no detours.

Granny was careful to hop from bush to bush and house to house so they wouldn't discover that she was following them. They sharply turned into an alley behind AbStract. Granny stopped short and peeked around the corner. Waiting for the shysters was Baskerville!

Granny watched as they stepped to the short brick wall that covered a space in between AbStract and the next building. It was ridiculous but it was as if Baskerville was the lookout. First Fish disappeared into a hole in the wall in between the buildings, the little white poodle, Furball and Tank followed Fish. Granny moved forward to peer into the hole only to be stopped by Baskerville.

"Baskerville, it's me, Granny. Want a treat?" Granny pulled out some dried bacon bits that she always carried in case of a dog emergency.

Baskerville muttered a low growl and wouldn't let Granny through.

"Ok, I get it," Granny said as she backed away.

Just then her cell phone started playing the theme from the old TV show *Dragnet,* the song Granny had put in her phone so she'd know Franklin was calling. She'd given Franklin her number in case he needed to reach her.

"Granny, did you neglect to mention that you might have buried something else?"

"No, just the wine and then I plunked the grass Sally gave me on top of the hole."

"Was anything else stolen from Rack's?"

"They had a lot of money stolen. Why?"

"Because some of it's buried with the wine."

Granny dropped the phone in shock. She could hear Franklin yelling into the phone. Slowly she picked it back up.

"It wasn't there when I buried the wine. I swear it wasn't there!" Granny proclaimed.

"Well, it's here now. Granny, do you remember anyone visiting you besides the Big Guy after you buried the wine?"

"No, I told you I must have fallen asleep and the shysters licked my face to wake me up. No one else was there. Do you suppose the Big Guy buried the money and is framing me?"

"Granny, let's take this one step at a time."

"I know my next step. I have to figure out a way to find the shysters. I'm going into AbStract to nose around the outside wall next to the space between the buildings where I last saw the shysters."

Franklin yelled into his phone, "Granny, I don't think that's a good idea. Granny?"

Granny had already hung up the phone and proceeded to enter the store. Again, Granny wondered if Franklin had planted the money. Maybe her people reading skills were getting forgetful too.

"Morning, Justine," Granny said as she passed the jewelry counter, "any news about Estelle?"

"No, Granny, she just disappeared and everyone's looking for her. They think all four of the women who disappeared had a plan and planned the heists together. Who would have thought?"

"Keep the faith, Justine; we'll get to the bottom of this."

Granny looked up and there was the good looking young man staring at her from the back nook of the store. Granny started to head towards him when the Big Guy stopped her.

"Let me go. That young man who I keep seeing was over there." Granny pointed and the Big Guy followed with his eyes.

"There's no one there, Granny. I wanted to tell you that we can't rule you out as a suspect so if there's anything you want to tell us, now, would be a good time."

"I'm just a feeble old woman, Big Guy," Granny said in her weakest voice, "How would I make a forest disappear? Could you help me back to the chair in that corner? I think I need to rest a spell. All this hoopla is wearing me out." With that she extended her arm to him.

The Big Guy escorted Granny to the chair but before he left he said, "We'll be talking."

Granny pretended to sniffle at his words. Once she was sure he was out of sight, Granny started examining the corner. Everything appeared to be fine. Where did that young man go? Could she have imagined him?

As Granny turned, her umbrella hit the bottom corner where the walls met. Before Granny knew what was happening, the floor slid open, tumbling Granny through the floor and down some stairs.

Chapter Sixteen

Luckily, Granny's big pocketbook landed underneath her and broke her fall. Granny found herself lying flat on her back staring up at a ceiling that had now closed. Where was she and what had happened?

Granny slowly moved her toes, her arms and her legs. Yup, she seemed to be in one piece. Granny sat up and looked around. Strange, she didn't have trouble seeing at all. There seemed to be small glow lights lighting up whatever this tunnel was.

Granny was thankful she'd left her heavy duty, spiked umbrella at home or she could have ended up at the bottom of the steps looking like a popsicle on the end of a stick.

At the end of her toes were stairs leading up to the floor that she'd just fallen through. Granny stood up and dusted herself off, turned around and glared into the soft lighting. There seemed to be wide tunnels everywhere. The tunnels were lined with bricks on the floors and the walls. This area was almost like an underground street. Granny walked a little further. There seemed to be stairs leading up to other places in the distance. Granny started to walk towards them when she heard little paw clicks such as claws touching the brick walkways.

It was Fish, little white poodle, Furball and Tank and they were climbing the steps not too far from where Granny was. They didn't see her. She hurried over to the steps but by the time she got there, they were already through the hole in the wall.

Granny hurried back to the steps that led to the floor that she had fallen through. She would investigate the rest of the tunnels later. She climbed the steps and pushed on the floor. It didn't budge.

Meanwhile, Franklin, concerned about Granny's disappearance, since she wasn't answering her phone and he couldn't find her anywhere, was questioning Justine at the AbStract jewelry counter.

"Have you seen Granny today?"

"She was just here. She talked to the Big Guy. Granny was feeling weak so he led her to the chair in the corner nook." Justine motioned to the corner. "She must have left because she's not there now. I'm sorry I didn't see her leave."

Franklin paced and muttered to himself, "What am I doing here? Did she ask for my help? No, she hung up on me. What am I doing here?

"Did you say something, sir?" Justine asked.

"Have you ever had someone drive you crazy?" Franklin barked at Justine.

Justine jumped back, afraid that Franklin was going to pounce. "Ah, well, ah, I can't say I have lately." Justine slowly lowered her arm down to be ready to hit the alarm in case she needed to call for help from this all of sudden crazed-sounding man.

"She's driving me crazy. She doesn't listen, always winking and secretive. What does she take me for? A fool? I don't even know her and she's driving me crazy." Franklin turned and started stomping toward the door.

Justine, looking relieved that she'd escaped what she might call an unusual encounter, moved her arm back to the counter. "I hope you find Granny."

Franklin stopped in his tracks, muttered something under his breath, took a deep breath and turned back into the store. Justine lowered her arm to the alarm again but Franklin walked over to the corner nook and sat down in the chair to ponder where he could next look for Granny.

Meanwhile, Granny was studying the floor underneath Abstract. She pulled from her purse her spyglass, called a magnifying glass by her friends, so she could get a better look at the floor. Her spyglass, as Granny preferred to call it, caught a tiny nail sticking out of the corner next to where the floor should have opened.

Granny pulled on the nail. It didn't budge. It seemed to be loose but it wouldn't come out of the wall. She didn't want to get caught on that tiny little thing if she ever could slide the floor over and get back out. She was losing valuable time. The shysters would be gone by now.

Granny accidentally pushed down on the nail as she was trying to remove it. The floor opened. Granny started climbing out. She looked up right into Franklin's astonished gaze.

Granny put her finger to her mouth to indicate to Franklin that he should hush and be quiet. Granny stepped out and grabbed Franklin's arm and said loudly, "I'm very glad you found me Franklin. I was so weak I couldn't move off the floor."

Justine, hearing the conversation, looked up and seeing Granny's weakness, hurried over. "Granny, I didn't see you lying on the floor. I'm so sorry the merchandise hid you. I can't see the floor from the jewelry counter. I thought you'd left. You should have called out. Are you ok?"

"It's quite alright, dear. You didn't know I was on the floor, must have passed out for a bit, when I woke up I was too feeble to call out. Franklin will help me now."

Granny grabbed Franklin's arm and started herding him out of the store. When they got outside, Granny quickly dropped his arm. "Did you see the shysters? You won't believe what I found. We can't talk here. By the way, how did you find me?"

"I knew you were going to get in trouble. Then you hung up on me. I hurried down here as fast as I could to try and stop you from whatever crazy stunt you were going to pull and I saw your car parked down the street."

"You couldn't have seen my car down the street. I left it at your house. I followed the shysters on foot."

"Take a look. It's right down here." He led Granny down the street to the red 57 Corvette.

Standing by the Corvette was Gram Gramstead. "There you are, Granny. I've been waiting for you."

Granny, seeing her car, was at first speechless. After she recovered from the surprise at seeing her car, she pinned Gram with a look that would scare even the shysters.

"As you can see, I'm here, so what do you want?" Granny asked in a crusty tone.

"I thought we could hang out together. Do some shopping. Have some girl chat."

Franklin saved Granny from having to answer. "Right now Granny and I have some important business to attend to. But we could all have dinner tonight at Rack's. I'd be so happy to have the pleasure of dining with two beautiful women." With that, he winked at Gram.

Granny glared at him and poked him in the ribs. Sputtering, she replied, "I'm busy."

"I took the liberty of canceling your appointment, Granny." With a quick grab, Franklin secured Granny's arm with his hand and started leading her away. "See you at 6:00 p.m., Racks Restaurant, Gram."

"Take your hands off of me," Granny yelled at Franklin. "Where are you taking me and why do we have to have dinner with that woman?"

"I'm taking you to Ella's Enchanted Forest to have a donut to sweeten you up. Then you're going to tell me why you came out of the floor at AbStract. We're having dinner with Gram because she seems to be new in town and we're going to get to know her. We need to know why she's following you." Franklin winked at Granny.

"That winking business is not going to work on me today, Franklin Gatsby. I have too much to do to try to keep myself out of the hoosegow. And I'm very annoyed with you." Granny stomped her umbrella on the ground to let him know she meant business and walked into the Enchanted Forest and sat down.

Franklin raised his hands and his eyes to the heavens, "Mama, did you come down and reincarnate yourself as Granny to drive me crazy? Or did you have a daughter you never told me about? There couldn't be two of you."

Franklin shook his head, sighed, and followed Granny into Ella's Enchanted Forest.

"Suppose you start telling me why you came through the floor," Franklin asked as he set the donuts on the table in front of Granny at the Enchanted Forest.

Granny hesitated for a moment, squared her shoulders for courage, and told Franklin the entire story of following Fish, little white poodle, Furball and Tank around the lake and behind AbStract. She told him the entire tale of not being able to follow the shysters because Baskerville was standing guard, and that's why she decided to investigate that wall of AbStract where she saw the good looking young man watching her. When she got to the part about falling through the floor, Franklin growled loudly.

"You should have called me before you investigated the wall, Granny. You should have waited for me. What if you couldn't have gotten out? I didn't know where you were. You could have been hurt. I understand why your kids are concerned. Do you ever listen to anyone?"

"If I listened to everyone, I'd be at the wrinkle farm harvesting my wrinkles. Look at it this way, if I couldn't have gotten out and no one could have found me, you wouldn't have to bury me."

Franklin ignored Granny's spurt of stubbornness. "So tell me what you saw down there."

After Granny finished telling him about the elaborate underground tunnels she found and the fact she saw the shysters in the tunnel, Franklin stood up. "I'm going to the courthouse to see if I can find out anything about when this town was built and why there might be tunnels underneath. Are you sure you haven't heard about this underground maze since you've lived in this area all of your life?"

"Not a word, if anyone would know I would. I know these stores like the back of my hand. Maybe I should go back in the tunnel."

"No, you do your usual rounds and see if you see anything suspicious. I'll pick you up at 5:45 at your house for dinner with Gram." Franklin turned and walked out the door.

Granny visited all her usual haunts but there was nothing unusual happening. Granny climbed into her red Corvette still wondering how it had gotten to Main Street. Had she driven it and imagined following the shysters around the lake on foot? Maybe she was imagining everything. Or maybe Franklin had driven her car to Main Street and he was the one playing tricks on her. She decided she needed to be careful.

Chapter Seventeen

Fish, the little white poodle, Furball and Tank were waiting for Granny when she walked in the door. Furball jumped on her head and started purring. Fish brushed against her legs happy to see her. The little white poodle was doing an excited dance and Tank was standing looking up at Granny holding an old key in his mouth.

Granny reached down and took the key out of Tank's mouth. It looked to be an old key, not one used in locks today. "So, is this what you shysters were doing in the underground tunnels?" Granny turned the key over in her hand, wondering if she should tell Franklin. She decided to wait until she snuck into the tunnels again and investigated them thoroughly. Maybe she'd find the lock that fit the key. And there was the fact that Franklin could have stashed the wine in her trunk and buried the money, trying to set her up. Granny wasn't going to be bamboozled by all of those cute winks.

Granny glanced at the clock. She supposed she had better get ready for what she was sure was going to be an excruciating evening in the presence of Gram Gramstead. Gram was so snoopy. Granny would have to watch what she said so she didn't give her predicament away.

When Franklin picked up Granny, she was dressed in her finest purple satin dress, her glittery purple loafers and her finest glittering, red and purple rhinestone earrings and necklace. She topped off her fashionable clothing with a red sequined beret. For a lark, Granny let her hair hang down to her shoulders with a few wisps curling around her earrings so they would be noticeable.

Granny ignored the wink Franklin gave her when he picked her up. After all, he seemed to be passing winks out without any consideration as to who he was winking at. If he could wink at Gram, then Granny didn't want any part of his winks. But Granny, being Granny, couldn't resist a little dig as she stepped out of her house and took Franklin's arm as he led her to his car. "What's the matter, Franklin, got a little twitch in your eye?"

Franklin ignored the jab and drove straight to Rack's parking lot and parked directly under the weeping tree on purpose, as it was getting dark and the tree was already starting to weep, hoping that maybe he and Granny would get trapped under the weeping branches. He thought it might make for an interesting night with Granny.

"I know what you're doing, Franklin, and it's not working." Granny quickly jumped out of the car. "You better move it or you'll be trapped all night, leaving me to take care of Gram all by myself," Granny snickered as she made a bee line for the door.

Franklin quickly pulled the car out from under the weeper and parked in a safe spot and sprinted after Granny.

Gram was waiting for them at Granny's favorite table. When they were seated and the waitress handed out menu's, Granny waited for Gram to take over the ordering like she did the last time Granny had dinner with her. To Granny's astonishment Gram put down the menu and said to Franklin, "I never know what to order. This large menu confuses me. Could you order for me please, Franklin?"

Granny started to sputter a response when she felt a light pressure on her foot. She looked at Franklin and he gave her that *let me handle this* look.

"Of course, I'll order for you. It's so nice to have a woman that likes to let a man take charge." And then he winked at Gram.

Granny pulled her foot out from under Franklin's quickly and kicked his ankle. "So, Gram, explain to us what brought you to Fuchsia? I hadn't seen you around until recently." Granny stared at Gram, trying to figure out why she thought she looked familiar.

"I moved here from Hollywood. I was a makeup artist. I got tired of the glamorous life and the parties so I decided I needed somewhere quiet and dull."

"You think we're dull?" Granny started to rise out of her chair, hand clenched around the umbrella handle.

Franklin quickly pulled Granny down and asked, "And do you find it as dull as you expected?"

"Yes, that's why I wanted to get to know Granny. I felt I needed to find a friend who I could bond with, enjoy life with. I didn't have time for that in Hollywood."

Granny rolled her eyes as Gretchen, the new waitress hired when Maizie disappeared, served them their food. Granny ate in silence thinking about the underground tunnels while Franklin and Gram flirted with one another.

All of a sudden, Gram jumped up, hurried over to the bar, swept her arm across the bar and knocked the salsa dip that a customer was dipping his chips in onto his lap. Gram then fell onto the man, knocking the bar stool and the man on the floor. She then stepped on the man with the tallest, sparkly high heels Granny had ever seen.

Granny couldn't believe what was coming out of Gram's mouth. Gram was uttering, "I'm sorry. I am so sorry. I'm just a clumsy old woman. Would you forgive me? I shouldn't have worn these high heels." She then pulled one of the high heels off of her foot and hit the man in the head. "Oh, no, I'm sorry it slipped in my hand."

When the last of those words came out of Gram's mouth, she dropped her pocketbook on his head as he was still trying to recover from the high heel to the head.

Granny's mouth dropped open and she started to get up. Franklin grabbed her, pulling her back down onto her chair. He then hooked his arm around the back of her shoulders to keep her from getting back up. Anyone looking at them would see a man hugging someone he cared about.

Out of nowhere, the Big Guy appeared. He hustled to the bar to diffuse the puzzling situation.

The Big Guy looked at Gram and the man still on the floor. "Are you ok, ma'am?"

"I'm fine for a feeble old lady. This man stole that man's wallet when he bumped into him." She pointed to the man sitting one bar stool away."

The man Gram was pointing at hurriedly checked his back pocket. "She's right; my billfold is gone."

The Big Guy checked the pockets of the man Gram had singled out. "It's here. Ma'am, you're a topnotch detective. What's your name?"

"Gram Gramstead. I'm happy to meet you. If you ever need any sleuthing assistance I'm your woman." Wearing a huge grin, Gram proceeded back to the table where Granny and Franklin were sitting.

Granny could barely keep it together. This Gram Gramstead was trying to steal her job. Granny wanted to reach over and pull her bright red, fake colored hair right out of her head but Franklin had too tight a grip on her shoulders.

"Well Gram, you must be tired after all that work. Can we drive you home?"

"No, I have my own car. Thanks for the dinner. It was exciting. We'll have to do it again sometime." Gram looked deeply into Franklin's eyes and said, "Perhaps just you and I?" With that, Gram winked at Franklin and walked out the door.

Granny started sputtering. "There's something about that woman that makes me want to scream."

"Maybe that's because she's a lot like you. She even looks a little like you the way she dresses and wears her hair. She can grab a crook with the best of them, Granny. Her red hair makes her stand out and call for attention. Maybe you should team up."

Granny pinned Franklin down with a glaring look, picked up her pocketbook and her umbrella and stated "Take me home." With a sharp pounding of her cane with each step, she walked to the front of the restaurant, winked at a cute waiter, walked out the door of Rack's and sat in the back seat of Franklin's car so she wouldn't have to ride in the front seat with him.

When Franklin walked Granny to the door of her house against her protests, he asked, "And what are you going to be up to tomorrow?"

Granny, thinking about the key that Franklin didn't know about, replied, "Dying my hair bright pink, since everyone seems to think bright hair makes someone smarter!" Granny retorted in a belligerent tone. Realizing that wouldn't get her what she wanted, she meekly lowered her eyes, sagged a little and yawned. "I'm so tired. I think I've had enough excitement for the week. I'm going to stay in bed and rest, eat chocolates and read a good book. There's no need for you to check on me. I'll be sleeping from time to time." Granny gave him another tired, meek look and walked in the house.

Granny decided to get a good night's sleep because she was going tunnel hunting tomorrow.

Chapter Eighteen

A rustling in the kitchen woke Granny up from a wonderful dream where the mayor of Fuchsia was presenting her with a key to the city and proclaiming it Granny Day for all of the crime in the city she had prevented.

Granny checked her attire. She'd gotten dressed last night and slept in her clothes so she could get an early start. She had the correct attire on so she jumped right out of bed to check out the noise.

Thor greeted her when she entered the kitchen. "Hi, Mom, I hadn't heard from you. What kind of trouble are you getting into now? I've heard rumors."

"You didn't tell your sisters did you?"

Thor ignored the question and set donuts down in front of Granny. "Now talk," he said in a stern voice.

"I've met someone." Granny said, thinking quickly.

"Someone?"

"A nice older man. You might say I fell for him."

"Those aren't exactly the rumors I heard. I heard that you might be having a few problems."

Granny looked at him with a guilty expression.

"I've heard you've been attacking strangers in stores claiming they've stolen something, only they've been innocent. Do we need to take you to a doctor?"

Granny, relieved that this was all he'd heard, sighed and said "Why don't we give it a few weeks and see how I'm feeling. It only happens occasionally. If it doesn't stop, I'll let you take me to the doctor. Maybe it's time for the wrinkle farm."

Thor gave her a suspicious look, kissed her cheek and started for the door. "Oh, and, mom, maybe the next time you'll explain to me how you happen to all of a sudden have a forest in your back yard. And don't worry, I won't tell your daughters that you now have four creatures living in your house. I also stocked your freezer with ice cream." He winked at his mom and walked out the door.

Granny got her umbrella and her pocketbook ready. She loaded her pocketbook extra heavy in case she ran into any problem in the tunnels. She remembered to check on her neighbors. George was certainly getting creative with his boxer shorts these days. They were always different colors and you never knew the strange ways they were going to be hung on the pole. She'd ask George later what was happening with that. He was always so neat.

Granny decided to walk to town. She didn't want anyone, especially Franklin, to see her car. He didn't need to know what she was up to. She wasn't sure yet if she could trust him. Anyone who would flirt with Gram wasn't trustworthy in her book.

Baskerville was sitting outside, guarding Mrs. Shrill's house. Granny decided Baskerville needed some donuts, so she'd saved some from the plate Thor had brought to her. She tossed the donuts at Baskerville and, right on cue, Mrs. Shrill showed her face outside the door and shook her finger at Granny and said, "Tut, tut, tut."

Granny threw her a donut and laughed at the look on Mrs. Shrill's face as she caught the donut. It made Granny so happy, she skipped all the way to AbStract.

Justine was at the jewelry counter when Granny entered AbStract.

"Hi, Granny, anything I can help you with today?"

"No, just nosing around. Continue with polishing those gems." Granny pretended to be examining the purses near the nook at the back of the store. When Justine wasn't looking Granny hurried over to the nook and gave a good crack at the corner with her umbrella.

This time Granny was ready. She quickly stepped aside as the floor opened and then proceeded down the hidden stairs. The floor automatically closed behind her.

Granny's eyes adjusted quickly to the mellow lighting in the walkways. As Granny looked around, she thought it looked like a street straight out of Harry Potter. It was strange because it was very clean, as if a street crew had been maintaining it. Granny walked to the steps where she'd seen Fish, the little white poodle, Furball and Tank enter and exit the hidden underground world. She climbed the steps and peered out the hole.

It appeared that this had once been an exit in between AbStract and its adjacent building. It would have led to main street had it not been blocked off. Granny turned around back down the steps and walked the distance which she guessed to be almost a block.

There were stairs leading up to another closed floor. Granny didn't try to find the entry; she kept on walking forward on the underground street. There were more stairs at intervals leading up to other floors of some type of buildings.

As she walked further, there were no more stairs but the streets led into more streets branching off of the main underground brick-lined walkways. Granny walked them all until she came to a dead end. She would then turn around and walk down another walkway.

At intervals, Granny found indentations in the wall. She was able to slide one over a little to reveal a door. Granny was able to squeeze her little hand inside the slit and feel a lock. She took the key and tried it in the lock but it didn't fit.

Granny didn't know how long she spent in the tunnels, but as she was walking down the final underground street, she felt something land on her head. It was Furball and with her was Fish, the little white poodle and Tank. She sat down on the ground and petted and greeted them.

"So, this is where you hide out? What is this place?"

At that question, Furball jumped off of Granny's head. Fish, the little white poodle and Tank ran with Furball down the underground street out of sight.

Granny wondered about the time. She'd left her cell phone at home in case there were creepy people down here. She was always forgetting to turn it to vibrate and if it rang, she didn't want to be caught trespassing in the creepy people's lair. Granny couldn't remember where she'd left her watch.

Granny gave a chuckle as she moved the nail to open the floor at AbStract. She hoped no one was standing on the floor or sitting in the chair by the floor opening. She'd hate to give someone a heart attack and be put in the orange jumpsuit for that.

The coast was clear. In fact, it was very clear. The store was closed. Granny glanced up at the clock on the wall. It was after 5:00. The streets rolled up early in Fuchsia. Now she was in a dilemma. How was she going to exit the store without setting off the alarms?

Granny decided she'd call Franklin to rescue her. After all, maybe he had found some information on the town that would explain the tunnels. She'd still keep her key find to herself. First, she had to find a phone. It would be the last time Granny left home without her cell phone.

Granny happened to glance out the window. There was the good looking young man and he was looking straight at her. Granny smiled and waved at him, thinking the tables were turned. He was usually inside and she was usually outside. However, that didn't solve her dilemma. Where was a phone? And if she used the phone would it set off the alarms so the store would know she was inside?

She could see the orange jumpsuit becoming a reality and she didn't look good in orange.

The young man had disappeared. All of sudden, Franklin peered into the window as if looking for something. She waved at him. He gave her an exasperated look and shook his head. He shouted through the window, "I'm calling the store manager."

Granny gave him an alarmed look until he said, "When he comes, hide. I'll get him to let me in and you can slip out unnoticed. But don't run away because I'll hunt you down if it's the last thing I do. You're the most exasperating woman!" He proceeded to take out his phone and make the call.

Granny hid behind the designer shoe shelves at the front of the store. She saw a pair of shoes exactly like the ones Gram Gramstead had been wearing at Rack's the other night. Gram couldn't be too poor if she could afford these shoes. Who was she?

The store manager let Franklin in the front door. Franklin led him back to the men's clothing department mentioning something about looking for his wallet in the dressing room. Granny quickly snuck out the front door and started sprinting for home.

She was almost to her driveway when Franklin pulled up beside her in his 1957 black Corvette. "Thought you could get away didn't you? You aren't going anywhere until you tell me why you were locked in tonight at AbStract. I happened to be looking for you. You were suspiciously missing today. I checked your garage and your car was there. To think I was actually worried about you. Resting? Resting!"

he shouted, "I should know better," Franklin chided Granny.

Granny gave up and invited him in. When Fish, the little white poodle, Furball and Tank saw them come in, they ran and hid underneath the bed in Granny's bedroom.

"Why do you suppose Itsy and Bitsy ran and hid from me?" Franklin asked in a bewildered tone.

"Because you call them Itsy and Bitsy," Granny answered with a sly smile on her face, "Let's get this over with Franklin. I'm tired and I want to go to bed. I investigated the tunnel and I found nothing. When I came up the steps and back into the store, it was closed for the evening. End of discussion. Did you find out anything about the underground streets and tunnels?"

"Not a thing. I checked the courthouse, old maps, new maps and the history of the town. It seemed the founding father of Fuchsia was Phineas Fuchsia. In fact, he built the house you're living in and the other old Victorian houses that pepper some of the neighborhoods. He owned and leased most of the businesses that started this town. He built the buildings and invited people in to start their own businesses. You could say he owned the entire town at one time. Your house was one of the original homes. The homes across the street from you such as Mavis,' George's and Sally's are part of the newer editions."

"It's time for you to go home, Franklin. I'm going to faint from exhaustion." Granny took his arm, led him to the door and closed it in his face. She half expected him to knock to try and get back in and she was kind of disappointed that he didn't. However, she had sleuthing to do.

Granny pulled out her maps of the city. She found AbStract and then started mapping her journey underground. The street and the steps all seemed to coordinate with the original buildings that Franklin had said were built by Phineas Fuchsia.

She had always known that AbStract, Ella's Enchanted Forest, Nail's Hardware, Rack's Restaurant, Lulu's Quilt Shop, Pickles Grocery, Headaches' Drugstore and Ecstatic Emporium were part of the old Fuchsia formerly known as the village.

In Granny's foggy brain, she felt that the underground streets, the good looking young man and the heists all had to be connected, but how? Had the women who worked in the stores who Granny had befriended been part of these heists?

Granny had always thought she was a good judge of character, but maybe her intuition was failing her in her granny years.

Fish, little white poodle, Furball and Tank came out from under the bed once Franklin had left.

"What's up with you four hiding? You like Franklin. Furball and Tank, he's your dad. Were you afraid he was going to take you home?"

Little white poodle took that moment to drop a note at Granny's feet speckled with drops of red. Was it blood? Granny picked up the note. Her big toe turned purple when she read the note. It said: "Help us please! We can't get out. We are being held hostage because of love. Help, please find us…. We don't know how much longer we have."

Chapter Nineteen

Granny started shaking and dropped the note. After she calmed down, she picked the note back up and examined it carefully.

"Where did you get this note, little white poodle? I wish you could talk."

Granny sat down on the couch and looked at the note, looked at the maps and looked at the four shysters. Then she got up and started pacing back and forth, back and forth, and back and forth.

When she was done pacing, she went over to the fridge and pulled out the ice cream. She scooped a big bowl of ice cream, loaded it up with crumpled chocolate donuts with sprinkles and then drizzled chocolate syrup on the top. She sat down and examined the maps some more.

Should she call the Big Guy and tell him about the note? Would he think she was involved? Would he take her seriously?

If she didn't call, what would happen? Would the women turn up dead because she didn't tell someone?

A drop of chocolate flirted with her map. It made a spot right at the end of her street. Chocolate always did solve Granny's problems. That drop of chocolate gave Granny an idea.

Granny gathered up her maps, found her umbrella and dug out her lantern. Granny then proceeded in the dark to the forest in her backyard where she got her crowbar and her shovel. She put all of her gathered items in the trunk of her 57 red Corvette.

Granny quietly drove into the alley behind AbStract. Normally, Granny ignored alleys at night. Nothing good ever happened in alleys on television shows and Granny was scared of rats and she was sure she'd step on a rat in some dark alley on some dark night.

Granny parked in front of the closed brick wall with the hole between the buildings. Granny checked out the alley to make sure she was all alone. Nope, no rats, not even the human kind. Granny opened the trunk and took out her crowbar, her hammer that she kept in the trunk, and her shovel. She laid them by the hole in the wall. She then went back to the car for her lantern and her umbrella. She'd left her pocketbook at home so she didn't have so much to carry.

Granny was a little bit of a thing, but she still had muscles at her age thanks to her weight lifting in her basement three times a week. She brushed off the bricks and peered into the hole.

Then she gently tried to wiggle each brick around the hole to see how loose they were.

Granny picked up her hammer and gave a swing with all of her muscles behind it. It hit the top bricks full on. They came loose. She then took her crowbar and dug into the crumbling cement and pulled. The bricks fell one by one at Granny's feet.

Granny stood up and peered around her car, making sure no one heard the ruckus. She continued to pick away at the bricks until she had a hole big enough for her to crawl through. Granny being so tiny didn't have to break away too many bricks.

Granny put her tools back in the trunk and proceeded to crawl through the hole to the stairs on the other side. Once she got to the bottom of the stairs she pulled out the map from her pocket.

Granny was surprised that she didn't need the lantern. The underground streets were still lit with a mellow light. She might have to be careful. Night time was always the time the break-ins occurred so the creepy thieves might be ready for another heist and she didn't want to surprise them. She might end up in the cemetery if she did. She thought by the look of the map that it was possible that one tunnel led to the cemetery behind the fence at her house.

Granny proceeded to the steps of AbStract. Looking at the map, she followed the tunnel to where she thought Headache's Drugstore should be located. Headache's was also one of the original buildings in Fuchsia. Sure enough, there were steps leading to the drugstore. Granny climbed the steps, found the nail and pushed. The floor opened up over her head.

Granny peeked her head through the floor. It was Headache's Drug Store alright. Granny decided not to go into the drug store, but to proceed on to prove her theory. It appeared to Granny that these underground streets had access to all the first built buildings in town. That is the way the crooks were gaining access to the stores.

Granny stopped when she got to Ella's Enchanted Forest. Next to the steps was an indentation, something like a parking garage. Granny walked into the indentation and shined her lantern at the ceiling. The ceiling seemed to be one big block of floor cut out. Along the side of the wall were trolley's or railings attached to the floor as if it could be moved up and down.

In her mind, Granny was imagining the Enchanted Forest layout. This floor would be right where the forest had been in Ella's Enchanted Forest. Was this the way the forest had been stolen? If that was the case, how did they get the forest to Granny's back yard?

Granny decided to leave those thoughts for later and continued with her map, marking stairs with the stores on the map. She then headed down one of the underground streets that led away from Main Street. If her calculations were right it should be her street that she was on. She was a straight shot from Main Street.

On the way, she also marked the places in the wall that seemed to have sliding panels to doors. Later, she'd walk the streets from above and see if she could identify any old houses on the street.

When Granny got to where she thought her house should be, she found there was no panel, but looking closer she saw that one of the bricks seemed to be loose. She pulled the brick out to see the outline of a door behind the brick. Just at that moment, Granny heard hurried footsteps down the street.

Granny quickly jumped against the wall and peered down the long street. She saw a man scurrying down the street. Granny's eyesight was not what it used to be. From this distance, the man almost looked like the good looking young man who had been watching her.

It dawned on Granny that he was the one who was carrying off the heist and possibly had kidnapped Estelle, Hermione, Ella and Maizie. Granny got her umbrella ready in case she had to defend herself. She had to find a way out or hide in case he came this way. She couldn't go back to the hole or he might see her.

Granny saw there was one more street leading away from her street. Maybe it wasn't her street. She didn't have a street in back of her house, just a cemetery that had access from the other direction.

Granny never was very good at directions, so maybe she was all turned around. Whatever! She had to get out of there. Granny started down the unknown underground street only to come to a dead end and another place hollowed out as if it was a parking space. This time the parking space had a floor with what appeared to be a lift on it. Where was she? There were no old buildings on the map she had.

Granny walked over and stood on the lift and looked at the ceiling. There was no way out of here. She couldn't see any lever to move the lift. Besides that, Granny had no idea where the lift would take her to. It might take her straight to the crooks and she had left home unarmed without her pocketbook.

As Granny started to move off of the lift she accidently tripped over a brick lying on the side of the lift. All of sudden the lift started moving. Granny fell back, knocking her hat off and leaving her staring at a ceiling that moment by moment was getting closer to her head.

Granny covered her head, issued a prayer and wondered what her children would think when they found her squished between this contraption and the floor. Or maybe they wouldn't find her and they'd think she'd wandered away in her fogginess never to be found again.

Granny could imagine the epitaph on her tombstone; this is where Granny should be, she left us nothing but a key. Nobody was found, her mind wasn't sound, is Granny still wandering around?

Just as Granny was ready to be squished, the floor opened up and Granny found herself in a big stone building. Granny rolled off of the lift onto a stone floor. The lift moved back down into the underground street and the floor closed up as if by magic.

Granny, still in shock that she hadn't been squished, brushed herself off and stood up. She hadn't quite realized yet that her way of escape, the floor, had sealed her into the cement structure. It was dark and dim. A little light filtered in through the windows at the top of the stone structure.

Where was she? She thought she could make out statues or pillars in the dimness of the light shining in through the windows. Seeing the light, Granny realized she'd been underground all night.

Granny walked around the walls of the structure. She came to a door, but it was locked from the outside. She turned and examined the large stone sitting in the middle of the structure surrounded by other smaller stones. At first, she'd thought they were statues but then she realized they were grave stones. The only one that was a statue was the large one and the statue was on top and reached almost to the ceiling.

She looked closer at the larger gravestone and was able to make out the name on the gravestone. Carved in the stone was the name Phineas Fuchsia, founding father of Fuchsia, Minnesota, and decided the statue on top must be a statue of Phineas.

Granny's heart started beating faster than it had in a long time. She could smell and taste an end to the mystery that had been plaguing her. She had to get out of here.

Granny remembered she'd put her cell phone into her pocket on this adventure and made sure she had turned it to silent. She looked at her phone, "Drat, no signal." Granny realized the stone walls were blocking her signal but she had to try to find someone to get her out. Who should she call? Not her children. She'd be in the wrinkle farm faster than she could wrinkle her nose. Maybe she should call Mavis. There was no use dragging her into this mess. Granny had no idea how dangerous this could be.

Granny decided to call Franklin. She didn't know if she trusted him, but he did know about the underground streets and he might help her out, even if he was in with the thieves, to find out how much she knew. But first she had to figure out how to get a signal.

Granny walked over to the grave stone and statue of Phineas Fuchsia. She had on her sneakers. It had been years since she'd been rock climbing. Granny decided to try it. She remembered her mother's advice. "If you fall down, you pick yourself up." Granny hoped that if she fell down, she'd still be able to pick herself up because Phineas was way tall! But there was a window by his head.

Granny hiked up her skirt, grabbed his shoe and hoisted herself up. She put one foot on his hand, another on a button on his shirt and continued to climb until she sat on top of his head.

Granny hoped risking her life was worth it. Yup, she had a signal.

"Franklin," Granny shouted into the phone, "I know how the forest got into my back yard. You have to help me; I'm entombed in the cemetery behind my house."

Franklin could barely hear Granny even if she was shouting. "You say you have no room in your house?"

"No, I'm entombed in the mausoleum in the cemetery behind the fence at my house. I can't get out." Granny shouted.

Granny heard no more as she heard the telephone disconnect. She could only hope Franklin took her seriously and could save her.

Granny carefully climbed down the statue, only getting caught once on the end of Phineas' tie. It took her a few seconds of dangling before she was able to get a foothold again on a button and climb the rest of the way down. Granny patted herself on the back when she was down on the ground. "Not bad climbing for an almost old woman," Granny proclaimed out loud to the other tombstones.

While Granny was waiting for Franklin, she checked out the other tombstones. This must be the place where all the descendants of Phineas Fuchsia were buried.

Granny hadn't paid too much attention to this side of the cemetery. Usually when she attended a burial it was in the new part of the cemetery by the highway. She knew of the mausoleum, but since there didn't seem to be any more relatives from the Fuchsia family, no one visited this remote area of the cemetery.

Granny heard a creaking and a rattling of the door. Soon she heard a banging and something scratching and pulling at the lock on the mausoleum. That didn't seem to be working. She wanted to call out but she wasn't sure it was Franklin and she didn't want anyone to know she was here in case it was the crooks.

A loud bang echoed throughout the Mausoleum, followed by more bangs. It sounded like a car was back firing but then Granny realized it was gun shots. Granny quickly decided to make use of Phineas' big hulk of statue to use as a shield. She quickly looked around for something to attack her attacker.

At that moment, the door popped open and Franklin fell into the mausoleum. Granny ran to help him up. He started sputtering at her. "What have you gotten yourself into this time? You could've been killed or slathered or something. How did you get in here?"

"What were you trying to do, shoot me?" Granny yelled as she jumped out from behind the statue ready to sling the rocks she'd picked up from the ground.

Franklin picked up his gun off of the floor where it had fallen when the doors had popped open. Granny quickly jumped back behind the statue and started slinging rocks.

"Granny, stop!" Franklin yelled, as his big stature tried to hide behind one of the tinier gravestones to shield himself from Granny's onslaught of rocks. "How did you think I was going to get those locks off quickly. Call the locksmith and say what? Come quickly, Granny is entombed in the mausoleum?"

"Take the bullets out and slide them across the floor or I'll pelt you till you're lumpy," Granny yelled.

Franklin took the bullets and slid them across the floor. "Granny, this is ridiculous. I knew you were trouble with a capitol T."

"Now the gun, Franklin."

Franklin slid the gun on the floor towards Granny.

"Ok, you can come out now, I won't hurt you." Granny told Franklin. "Just wanted to be sure you weren't the crookster."

As Franklin came out from behind the smaller gravestone, Granny took his arm and hurried him out of the cement building. She walked him over to the fence that surrounded her back yard. It had already been in place when she bought the property.

"Franklin, how did you get here?"

"I went around to the highway and followed the remote road in to this part of the cemetery."

"Help me look for a large gate hidden in this fence line." Granny instructed him.

"How about I just haul you into my car and take you home and lock you in your house for your own safety? Or better yet, call your children and tell them to lock you in your house and throw away the key? Or better yet, send you to the wrinkle ranch," Franklin yelled, exasperated that again he'd gotten pulled into Granny's hijinxes. She was the most maddening creature he'd ever met next to his mother.

"Franklin." Granny batted her fake eyelashes at him. She'd put them on to see what it would feel like to sleuth like those sexy women in the movies, but she drew the line at wearing high heels like the detective women in the movies. "Franklin, I can't do this without you. I'm just his tiny little old woman trying to do my part with the little time I have left on this earth." Again, Granny batted her fake eyelashes and let a little tear run down the side of her face. It was good Franklin didn't see the little pinch Granny gave to her nose to make her eye water. It was a trick she'd learned when she wanted to get her brothers in trouble when she was young.

"I know all the tricks, Granny, I learned from the best of them. Batting your eyes and pinching your nose isn't going to work. However, I was a New York detective and once a detective, always a detective. For that reason and that reason only, I'm going to help you." Franklin couldn't believe those last words came out of his mouth; it was almost as if he couldn't help himself, as if someone was putting the words in his mouth. Again, he found himself helping Granny when he had no intention of helping Granny.

Granny hid the smirk on her face and turned to the fence.

They both searched the fence line when Granny noticed the vines covering the fence had been tampered with. She pulled back the vines to reveal a gate big enough to drive a large truck through. Granny had never noticed it because the vines also covered her side of the fence. Granny used all her weight to push open the fence gate. When it wasn't budging, Franklin added his brawn and the gate popped open.

"This is the way the forest got into my back yard."

"I think you're dreaming, Granny. How did the forest get from the Enchanted Forest to here?"

"See that side of the mausoleum? If you look closely, it's fake cement. I think there's a large door on this side of the building."

Franklin walked over and examined the wall. "There does appear to be a hidden garage type of a door here," Franklin concluded. "But that doesn't explain the forest."

Granny stepped through the gate. "Franklin, go get your car and meet me at my house." With that, Granny disappeared into her yard.

Chapter Twenty

Granny let herself in her back door and headed straight for the basement, not wanting to waste time waiting for Franklin to arrive.

Once in the basement, Granny eyed the wall that would be closest to the underground streets. She carefully examined her bookshelves. Nothing seemed out of the ordinary. She then gave all of her attention to the faux fireplace on the wall. The fireplace was a beautiful focal piece, but she'd always wondered why someone would put in a fake fireplace. In fact, a few years ago, Granny had contemplated replacing it with a real fireplace.

Granny closely examined the panel on the side of the faux fireplace, running her fingers on the edge of the expensive, carved thick wood paneling. She'd always thought the edges of the paneling were molded and carved for beauty, but now she saw that possibly it was made for movement.

Granny had never stuck her hand inside the fireplace, but this time she ran her fingers around the edges and deep in the recesses of the inside walls. She felt a latch hidden in the recesses on the right hand side, top corner. With one flick of the finger, the latch let loose. One side of the fake fireplace popped open from the wall. Granny stepped back and grabbed hold of the mantle and swung the fake fireplace front all the way open. She could not believe her eyes. Behind the fake fireplace front was a door. Granny cautiously opened the door. She peered into the darkness. Behind the door was a room.

Granny quickly grabbed the flashlight that she kept by the fireplace in case of a power outage.

As Granny swung the flashlight around the room, she saw that it was approximately 10 by 10 feet wide by 12 ft. tall. Granny walked into the room.

The room had a few cobwebs, which was surprising, since it appeared to not have been disturbed in many, many years. The walls were bare. These walls were concrete, unlike the walls of the underground streets. There was no furniture in the room.

At the other side of the room, Granny's flashlight hit the shiny metal of a door. Granny knew it was the door that led to the underground streets. Granny walked over and pulled on the door. The door was not locked. It was stiff from years of being blocked up and not opened, but as Granny tugged on the handle, it gave way to the brick wall on the outside that Granny had examined earlier. Granny could see where she had pulled out the brick the night before, because the mellow light from the underground street gently shined through the hole like a bright star in the night.

Granny started to work on the bricks. Surprisingly, she could take them out by hand. They seemed to have been set in on top of one another with very little mortar around them. Granny was almost through to the other side when she heard the doorbell ring and pounding on the door upstairs.

Thinking Franklin was finally here, Granny ran up the stairs and pulled open the door, excited to tell him about her latest find.

"Franklin, you won't believe….." Granny stopped in mid sentence when she saw her visitors.

"Granny, we have a search warrant for your house." The Big Guy handed her the warrant and stepped into her house followed by two policemen.

"Why now and why my house?" Granny asked in a feigned bewildered tone.

"There was another robbery last night, Granny. Persnickety's Bookstore. Again, it appears it was an inside job. The only difference this time is that no one has disappeared. Ditty Belle closed up as usual. She left her cat Snuffles in the bookstore for the night. This morning she found Snuffles outside her door. Someone had let Snuffles out. Then she discovered that all her books had been stolen. Some of them were very rare editions worth a lot of money."

"And how does that have anything to do with the search warrant on my house?" Granny asked with an uppity tone.

"Your car was found in the alley behind AbStract this morning. Can you explain why your car has been parked on the street near the crime scene every time there's been a heist? And can you explain the forest in your backyard? A concerned citizen reported there was unusual greenery in your yard when she was out for her daily walk."

"And who might that be?" Granny practically shouted at the Big Guy as she marched up to him and started tapping on his chest with her finger.

Big Guy pulled back and looked at Granny with a piercing intensity.

"Mrs. Shrill. She said Baskerville got lost in the forest in your back yard, a forest that has never been there before. We checked and it does resemble the forest from Ella's Enchanted Forest."

Granny silently wondered what had happened to Franklin. "She's out to get me. Well, her tut, tut, tuts can't hurt me," Granny said in a sobbing tone. "I guess I'll go and sit in front of the fireplace in my basement, and cry and rest, while you tear up my house. You'll know where to find me."

Granny hung her head, put on her best martyr face, and slowly made her way down the stairs, making sure she had her umbrella with her.

Once she was certain no one had followed her, she quickly walked through the hidden door in the fireplace that she'd left open. Once inside, she pulled the door shut. Granny knew she had to save herself. Everyone was conspiring against her and it would be an orange jumpsuit or the wrinkle farm faster than she could raise her umbrella if she didn't solve this puzzle.

Hiding in the underground streets would give her time. Granny walked over to the metal door, took out a few more bricks and crawled through the opening she'd made in the bricks. As Granny did this, she wondered if she'd ever see her house or the light of day ever again. There was no going back. She'd wait and confront the thieves. Granny felt something sticking into her side from her pocket. It was the key. She had forgotten in her fogginess that she still had the key. Looking at the key Granny knew what she had to do.

Chapter Twenty One

Granny took the key out of her pocket. She had to find the door that fit the key. It had to have something to do with why she had the earrings that were stolen from AbStract and why she had the earrings that the girls had been wearing on the nights they'd disappeared.

Granny decided she had to check all doors on the side streets off of Main Street. She hadn't had the time to map out who lived where and who matched up to the hidden doors behind the panels in the underground street. Perhaps there were more doors but they were bricked up and she hadn't noticed them.

Granny slowly started walking toward the underground Main Street, being vigilant about running into the crooks. She had only made it about a block when she noticed an indentation of a panel in the bricks. Granny took her umbrella end and wedged it between the panel and the wall. Surprisingly enough, it moved easily as if it had been used recently. *Could it be this easy,* Granny thought.

Granny slid the panel sideways to reveal the metal door. Granny's hand was shaking as she put the key in the lock. Granny looked around to see if anyone was watching. It appeared she was alone on the street. Granny quietly, but quickly, unlocked the door. Granny held her breath as she slowly turned the knob. The door opened. Granny caught a whiff of perfume. Granny had a moment to recognize the smell. It was the smell of the flowers that she had in her hands the day they found her sleeping in her back yard. As Granny fell to the floor the look of surprise was still frozen on her face.

"Granny, Granny, wake up!"

Granny felt something cool and wet on her forehead. She felt again as if she was trying to wake up again from a long winter's nap. As Granny tried to open her eyes, she heard whispering.

"Do you think she's going to be ok? She is kind of old. Maybe her heart gave out."

"At least she doesn't have that surprised look still frozen on her face."

Granny gradually opened her eyes. "Am I dead?" she asked as she gazed into the faces of Estelle, Hermione, Ella and Maizie. "Are you dead?"

"No, Granny, we're not dead," Maizie replied as she helped Granny sit up.

Granny reached out her hand to touch each one of them to make sure they were not a figment of her imagination or that she wasn't really dead.

"You've all been missing. Now you're here. Where is here?" Granny asked in confusion.

"We don't know, Granny," Estelle said as she and Maizie helped Granny to her feet.

Granny dusted herself off and looked around. It was a small room similar to the hidden room in her house. This room was furnished with beds, a refrigerator, and a bookshelf in the corner filled with books.

"How did you get here?" Granny asked in a quiet voice, still a little foggy from her sleep

All four women answered as a chorus singing a woeful tune. "Love."

"Love?" Granny asked in consternation.

The four women burst into tears and started sobbing. Granny couldn't understand a word they were blubbering.

"Calm down, one at a time. This isn't a time for blubbering." Granny reprimanded the women, all the while holding back the inclination to join them in their blubbering. "First, are any of you hurt? I have a note with blood on it."

In between sniffs, Ella explained, "We managed to sneak the note out with the little white poodle. I was biting my fingernails so bad, they started bleeding while I was writing the note. We decided to leave it; if anyone saw the blood they might take the note seriously."

"Seriously! Seriously! You about gave this old girl a heart attack when I found it. Now back to the love."

"It started with me," Estelle explained. "I fell in love with this young, good looking, man who kept popping up at AbStract. He told me his name was Sonny. I never knew when he would show up. He seemed to appear out of nowhere. I never saw him enter through the front door, but all of a sudden he was always there; it was like magic. This was going to be my magical romance that I have always dreamed of. Sonny asked me out. He loved the earrings I wore. He took an interest in my job. When was the last time someone I dated cared about anyone but himself? He was so easy to fall in love with." Estelle let out a big sigh and burst into tears.

The other women rushed to her side to comfort her. After a brief moment, she was able to take a breath and continue. "One night I was closing up. I was supposed to meet Sonny later. I went to the front of the store to lock the door and when I got back to the jewelry counter, I found him taking the jewelry. He must have thought I'd left. All of a sudden, I smelled this perfume and I didn't remember anything more until I woke up in this room alone."

When Estelle finished, Ella continued the story. "Hermione met him next. She's been so traumatized that she hasn't been able to speak since she's been here. I must have met him after he sweet talked Hermione. He was always around a corner in the store surprising me. I kept Sonny a secret from my mother because I didn't think she'd approve. We started dating. He told me I was enchanting like the forest in my mother's store. No one had ever told me that before. It was so much fun to drive around in his 57 red Corvette convertible. It made me feel daring and alive."

At that confession, Granny's ears perked up. "He has a 57 red Corvette convertible?"

"Yes. I'd sneak out of the store and meet him in the alley and we would cruise the country roads. Then he would say that his time was up with the car and he had to get it back to the garage as it was a limited edition and he didn't like to keep it out after dark."

"Dark, schmark," Granny huffed, "He stole my car and made me think I was losing my marbles."

Ella continued, "Then one day, I was closing the Enchanted Forest for my mom. He'd made sure I would meet him at 8:00 p.m. at the lake so we wouldn't be found out. I locked the door and started for the lake, but I realized I'd left my car keys in the Enchanted Forest, so I walked back for them. When I entered the store, the entire forest was disappearing though the floor in the store. I thought I was hallucinating. Just as I was ready to call my mother, I smelled a whiff of perfume and that's the last thing I remember before I woke up in this room. Estelle and Hermione were already here."

Granny walked over to Hermione and patted her cheek. "Hermione, Hermione, you need to snap out of this. You weren't named after me for nothing. Don't tell anyone but my first name is Hermiony too and your mama named you after me because you were such a spitfire of a little baby. Your momma was my best friend in school. Don't let me down. We Hermionys don't give up. We don't give in and we aren't quiet."

Hermione gave a little sniff and looked up at Granny. "Was I really named after you? Mama died when I was so young. I feel so stupid. He promised me jewels and a puppy. I've never had a puppy." Hermione started wailing loudly.

"Hermione, we Hermionys don't wail; we don't fail; we send guys like him to jail."

"Well, that's not what happened to me," Maizie piped in. "Sonny was going to marry me. I was going to finish my shift at Rack's; we were going to climb into his semi- (he told me he drove a truck for a living) and ride happily off into the sunset, only somehow I apparently rode happily ever after into this room. All I remember is my shift being over. I was going to throw my suitcase into the back of his truck. When I opened the back doors, it was already full with wine and money. I remember smelling a whiff of perfume and the next thing I knew, I woke up in this room with someone throwing a glass of water in my face." She turned and glared at Ella, Hermione and Estelle.

"We had to wake you up somehow. You kept trying to kiss us when you were coming out of whatever," Ella smirked.

Granny walked around the room with an eagle eye. She noticed a door exactly opposite to the door in the underground street. "This is the door that's the clue to where we are." Granny started pulling on the door. It was locked.

Granny remembered she still had her key in her hand. She started to put the key in the lock when the door to the underground street opened. Standing in the doorway was the good looking young man. He pointed a big gun right at Granny.

"Hold it right there, Granny. Drop that key. You're not going anywhere."

Granny decided this was not a time for the faint of heart but it was a time for a faint. Instead of dropping the key, she dropped in the best Granny faint she could muster. It got everyone's attention. The women rushed over and caught her right before she was going to hit the hard ground. Granny kept her eyes closed but winked quickly at Maizie. She needed a little time to come up with a plan.

"Granny! Granny! Look what you've done, you've killed Granny," Estelle shouted.

You've given her a heart attack," Ella chimed in.

Hermione cried louder.

Maizie just kept patting her face.

"She's fine. Granny, get up. I know you're faking. I've been watching you for months."

"Sonny, how can you be so cold and heartless?" Maizie asked.

"She's a fraud. She's a fake. She works for the Big Guy. Get up, Granny," Sonny advised, as he pointed the gun directly at Granny.

"Since you put it that way," Granny raised herself up, letting the women lift her to her feet, and stomping her feet and her umbrella, "You won't get away with this."

Just then, the inside door opened. Gram Gramstead, in all her redheaded glory, rushed into the room.

"Gram, get out of here. Now your following me has really got you in trouble, run, get help," Granny yelled in exasperation.

"I don't think so, Granny," said Gram as she raised her umbrella in one hand and pointed a small gun at Granny with her other hand.

"Gram Gramstead, put that gun down," Granny ordered.

"No, Granny, this has gotten out of hand and it's your fault."

Granny straightened herself as tall as she could with her five foot frame and put herself in target's way.

"My fault! My fault!" Granny yelled in outrage as she got ready to raise her umbrella.

"I wouldn't try it, Granny, I'm on to your tricks. Remember, I've studied you and I know your every move."

Just at that moment, little white poodle ran in from the underground street door that had been left open.

"Hercules, where have you been?" the good looking young man said to the little white poodle, while still holding the gun on the three women.

Granny turned. "Hercules? That's little white poodle. Hercules? Please," Granny said in disdain.

"Sonny boy, don't let that wimp dog of yours, Hercules, distract you," Gram reminded him. "We have to change our plans now and get rid of these people, all because of her." Gram advanced on Granny, not taking her gun off of her target.

"Little white poodle is your dog?" Granny asked in disbelief, trying to ignore the gun pointing straight at her. "And you named him Hercules? What is the matter with all the men in town? They have serious naming ability problems. Don't you think, Gram?"

"Don't try to distract me. Sonny boy, tie them all up." Gram gestured to them all to move into the corner.

Just as Gram was gesturing, there was a loud bang and the door away from the underground street that led into the unknown building crashed open. Baskerville in all his bigness bounded into the room and attacked Gram Gramstead. While Gram was trying to fend off Baskerville, little white poodle started nipping on Sonny Boy's shins. At that moment, there was a ruckus at the door to the underground street and Furball bounded in and landed on top of Sonny Boy's head. Tank jumped on Sonny Boy's chest as Sonny Boy fell to the ground. Tank tussled with Sonny Boy's hand with his mouth. The gun flew into the corner. At the same time, Fish, coming through the door, gave a loud meow and ran over and dug his claws into Gram Gramstead's stockings to keep her from getting up from the floor where Baskerville had her pinned. Baskerville, at that moment, knocked the gun out of Gram's hand. It flew through the door to the unknown building. Then Baskerville opened his mouth wide and pulled Gram's hat and the bright red wig off of her head revealing..........

Chapter Twenty Two

"I knew you looked familiar, Mrs. Shrill!" Granny exclaimed in triumph. And that red hair isn't even real!"

The woman on the floor started struggling. Baskerville growled and put a big paw on the woman's head while Fish dug his claws into her clothes to keep her still. Granny instructed Maizie to pick up the gun in the corner, as she backed out the door to the unknown building to pick up the other gun that had slid through the door. As Granny was picking up the gun, she lifted her head and realized she was in a garage. Parked in the garage was a 1957 red Corvette.

Granny saw red and the red Granny was seeing wasn't the car. She stomped back into the room with the gun and pointed it at the woman lying on the floor.

"You, you stole my car again! Granny pointed her umbrella at the woman. Then Granny lifted the gun. Maizie, Hermione, Ella and Estelle gave a gasp, thinking Granny had lost it for good this time.

"Granny, perhaps you should put the gun down and we should do something, like call someone and tie these people up?" Maizie suggested hopefully.

"I'm not going to shoot them," Granny yelled in exasperation. Granny lifted the gun, took out the bullets and put them in her pocket. She told Maizie to do the same with her gun.

Seeing that the shysters had the two firmly in hand, Granny wanted some answers.

"You stole my car," Granny glared at the woman on the floor, tapping her umbrella near the woman's head.

"I didn't steal your car," moaned Mrs. Shrill. "I bought one just like it. Then I'd have Sonny Boy borrow your car once in awhile just to throw you off."

"Tut, tut, tut," Granny exclaimed as she shook her finger at Mrs. Shrill.

Mrs. Shrill continued, "You thought you were so clever. Everyone loved you. You'd prance around and save the day. You pretended to be this helpless old woman, and you kept spoiling Baskerville. Even he liked you better than me. I decided if you were sent to the wrinkle farm then I, Gram Gramstead, my new persona, could take over. Everyone would love me and you'd just be a crazy, forgetful old lady who no one trusted anymore. I didn't want anyone else to get hurt. But Sonny Boy here had other ideas when he volunteered to help me."

Granny walked over and tapped Sonny Boy in the leg, while still looking at Mrs. Shrill. "Who is he?"

"He's my hopeless son. He got out of prison a few months ago and decided he and that wimp of a white poodle, Hercules, were going to live with me. I told him if he was going to live with me, he had to work for his keep. He was going to help me make it look like you'd lost it, Granny. He was going to help me put you in the wrinkle farm, so I could take over your job and everyone would love me, not you. But he decided he wanted more."

Sonny Boy tried to raise his head to speak, but Furball hissed and jumped harder on his head.

"Furball, let him speak," Granny instructed the large cat.

Sonny Boy again raised his head, this time with Furball watching cautiously for any tricks. "You didn't think I was going to move a forest and do all this for no payback, did you, Ma? Besides, look at those women. It's too bad they caught me. I could have had it all, especially with Maizie. Jewels, electronics, money, rare books, the wine, if sold, would have netted me millions. Who would have thought a ratty tat restaurant would have had such an expensive stash of wine in its basement?"

"My grandfather, Phineas Fuchsia, built this town," shouted Mrs. Shrill in her shrill voice.

"It's my town. People had no clue who I am. I decided I was going to show them. I found my grandfather's journal and plans for the town hidden in a trunk in the basement. This was his house. I wanted it all."

Granny thought Mrs. Shrill was aptly named.

"When I found the plans and the underground streets," Mrs. Shrill continued, "I knew I was meant to do this. My grandfather's spirit was instructing me to continue his plans. According to his journal, he built the underground streets at the same time as he built the town. He paid his crews to be silent about the underground streets until he was ready to have them revealed. His vision was to have a town that could be accessed from both above and below ground. During the grueling winters, people could use the underground streets to get to the stores and their homes. He had left his wife and family back in New York. He was planning to bring them out when he was finished. He lived here by himself. Then he got sick, so even though the underground streets were built, he had them boarded up. He leased the buildings one by one, never revealing the other entrances. My father inherited this house from him but never visited. It was always rented out. I rented it out for many years too and then decided I needed some new scenery and so I moved to Fuchsia."

Gram, or Mrs. Shrill, whatever her name was, continued on, "My plans were not as noble as his. After I found the plans and investigated the streets, Sonny Boy and I cleaned them up. It was Sonny's idea to make a little money on the side too. It fit perfectly. We could set you up as the forgetful, spacey old lady who was behind it all. You'd go to the wrinkle farm because who would put a sweet, forgetful old lady who was having problems, in jail. We'd be rich from our spoils. The best part is no one would know."

"Then Sonny Boy started to have an eye for the ladies. They happened to get in the way. We locked them up here until we could deal with them."

All of a sudden, Maizie spoke up. She, Hermione, Ella and Estelle had been cowering in the corner trying to stay out of harm's way. Maizie stepped to the side of the girls with something in her hand. It was the gun Granny had told her to empty of its bullets. Maizie raised the gun.

"Sorry, Granny, I do like you, but I love Sonny more. We were going to live happily ever after as soon we tied up loose ends, meaning you and these other three twits who got in the way. You aren't the only undercover snitch here; I was a plant to keep these silly young girls under control. Let Mrs. Shrill and Sonny Boy go or I'll shoot each one of you one by one. I'll start with Ella." Maizie moved and grabbed Ella and held her close.

"And to think I entrusted my secret food cravings to you, Maizie. I'm crushed. Granny stomped her foot on the ground hoping Ella would get the drift.

"Granny looked at Ella's scared face and looked Ella straight in the eye. "Tank, Fish, little white poodle, Furball and Baskerville, come here now!" Granny instructed.

Just at that moment, there was a crash outside the door. Maizie swung towards the door. Ella stomped on Maizie's foot. Maizie screamed, hopped in pain, dropped the gun and let go of Ella. Franklin, the Big Guy and the entire Fuchsia police department stormed through the door from the underground street.

Fish and Furball started meowing as loud as they could. Tank, Baskerville and little white poodle started barking. Granny took her umbrella and hooked Gram/Mrs. Shrill's arm so she couldn't get away. At the same time, Franklin, quickly assessing the situation, grabbed the good looking young man now known as Sonny Boy, by both arms. Franklin finished subduing him by attaching Sonny Boy's wrists with handcuffs and hooking him to a pipe protruding from the wall.

The shysters were still barking and meowing the room down. "Enough shysters!" Granny shouted above the din. She glanced at Franklin just in time to see him wink at her. This time Granny winked back.

Granny took the time to comfort Estelle, Hermione and Ella and turn them over to three cute police officers who would escort them home.

After the Big Guy and the police hauled Mrs. Shrill, Sonny Boy and Maizie to their little room in the quaint Fuchsia jail, Granny turned to Franklin.

"How did you find us?"

"After I left you at the cemetery, I went back to the courthouse. I pulled up the history of the town. It baffled me as to how the forest got into your back yard. I noticed from old court records, that Ella's Enchanted Forest originally was a Funeral Home. You happened to have gotten stuck in a cemetery in a mausoleum. There had to be a connection.

I drove over to the Enchanted Forest and walked around the room where the forest had been. I checked out the nooks and crannies. When I gave one a tap, the entire floor descended into the underground street. That's how they transported the trees. The street is big enough for a truck. They drove a truck underground to the Enchanted Forest, loaded the trees and drove to the space near your house that has a lift that was formerly made to be able to lift the caskets into the cemetery. Phineas had planned on transporting the caskets underground from the funeral home to the cemetery mausoleum in the winter time.

Whoever was setting you up, used it to transport the forest of trees. Once they got the trees into the mausoleum they took them through the fence into your back yard. Once I figured this out, I rode the floor down to the streets. I then called the Big Guy. He had just noticed you were missing and he found the door you escaped through. You thought you'd closed it, but it didn't latch so the fireplace appeared to be hanging off the wall. You were gone and the Big Guy knew you hadn't gotten past him. He found the door at the same time that I called him, so he followed your path from that direction. I started from the direction of the Enchanted Forest. We found the door and you in time to hear the confessions."

"Oh, Franklin, I feel a little faint. All of this is too much for an old woman." As she made that statement Granny started edging out the other door that led to Mrs. Shrill's basement garage.

Franklin was about to follow, when Baskerville stood in front of the door and growled, stopping him in his tracks. Furball jumped on his head. "Itsy, what are you doing?"

"Franklin, haven't you learned anything yet, that is Furball. You men need to give these heroes respectable names." Granny took advantage of his confusion and slipped through the door, slammed it shut and locked it. She grabbed the keys off of the wall of Gram or Mrs. Shrill's garage and hopped into Mrs. Shrill's red 1957 Corvette. Opening the garage door, Granny checked the street for movement before she backed the car out of the garage.

After all that excitement, Granny needed to get out of town. She headed straight for Brilliant, Minnesota, and Red Hot Mama's Boutique. Granny spent the rest of the day picking out some spicy nightwear. It was time for a change. She'd spent too many nights lately in her clothes and trying to stay out of the hoosegow. It was time to add to her nighttime attire collection. She might be daffy but she wasn't dead.

When Granny arrived home, she parked her new, spare 1957 Corvette in the empty space in her double garage next to its twin 1957 red Corvette. As Granny walked to her door to enter her house, she heard howling that sounded like a four-footed furry creature was in pain. She found Baskerville sitting in front of the small pet door giving her his best sad face as he released a howl from deep inside his body. Granny laughed. "I guess I'm going to have to expand the pet door for you, Baskerville." Granny opened the door and let Baskerville in. Fish, the little white poodle, Furball and Tank were all waiting for her.

Granny set out two more big bowls for Baskerville and then fed the shysters their tofu, yogurt and vegetables while she pulled out ice cream and donuts for her dinner. She settled down in front of her television and enjoyed the news of the heists being solved. She especially liked the picture the news station used of her. Granny decided now that she was famous she might have to change her look a little so she could continue her undercover job. She wondered how she would look in red hair.

Granny was ready to give herself a facial with avocado's and lemon juice—after all, after a day like Granny had had, she needed a little tweak to her skin. Wrinkles were wrinkles, but wrinkles without avocados and lemon juice were really wrinkles. Just then, her phone rang.

Granny could hear the screeching on the other end before she could even shout, "What?"

"We just heard the news. You could have been killed. You could have been kidnapped! We'll be over tomorrow. We're going to talk about this!" both Penelope and Starshine said at the same time as they shouted into their speaker on their phone.

"It's not my fault. There was this man. His name was Franklin. He didn't tell me what I was getting into. He just asked me to help him and look what happened. I promise, I'll never help him again. He's a very bad influence." Granny pinched her nose hard so it hurt and made her sniffle. "You're right. I could have been killed." Granny gave herself another pinch. "My life flashed through my eyes and the thought that I might never see the three of you again scared me so much. I promise I'll never forget this lesson."

Granny gave a big yawn into the phone. "I have to go; I'm so tired. The stress, you know, but I'm fine. Please, don't worry. I just got caught up in something that wasn't my making."

"We're sorry we made you cry," Softhearted Starshine apologized.

"We'll talk about this, but when you're ready. We want to make sure you're ok. After all, you aren't getting any younger," Penelope reminded her.

"Sleep tight, mom," Thor advised his mother. "I've decided I'm going to move to Fuchsia. I'll be over soon to look for a house."

Granny jumped when she heard those words and slammed down the phone. She guessed it could be worse; it could be Penelope and her family—or Starshine—moving to Fuchsia. At least Thor wasn't so strict.

Granny changed into her new purple and red silk nightie accented with velvet lace and tiny pink bows around the neckline, and settled into bed. She fell asleep eating chocolates, reading her favorite hot novel and thinking how nice it was for things to be back to normal.

Chapter Twenty Three

The phone ringing early in the morning woke Granny as she was dreaming about Franklin putting a ring on her finger, while Fish, little white poodle, Furball, Tank and Baskerville watched.

"What now!" Granny screamed into the phone.

"10:00 o'clock, Ella's Enchanted Forest. Be there." With that, the caller hung up the phone.

Granny stared at the phone. The voice had sounded like Franklin's.

Granny peeked her big toe out from under the blanket. It was pink. It was going to be a warm day. It was a flip flop day. She listened to see if she heard any noises in the kitchen. It seemed her kids hadn't followed up with threatening to visit after their phone call last night. She hoped they missed the latest news last night too and didn't hear the reporters talking about Franklin as if he was the next best thing to Robert Redford dessert.

Granny decided it was safe to venture into her kitchen. There were no kid noises in the house. Granny grabbed her binoculars and decided she'd better check on her neighbors. She'd been a little remiss lately.

Granny trained her binoculars on George's house. There were no boxer shorts hanging on the pole. Granny started to grow concerned. She trained her binoculars on Mavis' house. Mavis' shade was pulled down and George's boxer shorts were hanging on the pole outside of Mavis house.

Granny got a sly smile on her face until she moved her binoculars to Sally's house. What she saw made her drop her binoculars and run out into the street, forgetting she still had on her purple and red, velvet trimmed nightie with pink bows on.

ABOUT THE AUTHOR

Julie Seedorf owns her own computer repair business, but her secret undercover job is writing. Her column "Something About Nothing" for a Minnesota newspaper is about nothing, which is what we talk about most of the time, always with something underneath the conversation. Julie has been a wife, mother, grandmother, housewife, barmaid, salesperson, activity director, full time volunteer and more. Her motto is, "If you dream it, you can do it." Her Fuchsia, Minnesota, series is the first of her journey in her undercover career. Having lived in small communities in Minnesota all her life, she knows the richness and uniqueness that only a small town can bring and with a little humor and imagination, she transforms those experiences into her imaginary Fuchsia community. Visit her Facebook page, *Sprinkled Notes*, find her on twitter @JulieSeedorf. Watch for her upcoming website.

WITHDRAWN

$14.95

LONGWOOD PUBLIC LIBRARY
800 Middle Country Road
Middle Island, NY 11953
(631) 924-6400
longwoodlibrary.org

LIBRARY HOURS

Monday-Friday	9:30 a.m. - 9:00 p.m.
Saturday	9:30 a.m. - 5:00 p.m.
Sunday (Sept-June)	1:00 p.m. - 5:00 p.m.

45740027R00119

Made in the USA
Middletown, DE
12 July 2017